We're All Mad Here

HELEN JULIET

We're All Mad Here

Copyright © 2024 by Helen Juliet

Cover Design by Joe Satoria

❀ Created with Vellum

BY HELEN JULIET

Contemporary Fairy Tale, Folk Tale and Classic Literature Adaptations

The Fairy Tale Collection Box Set (Beauty and the Beast, Cinderella, Rapunzel)

Daddy's Fairy Tales Box Set (Daddies and kink – Goldilocks, Little Red Riding Hood, The Three Little Pigs, Puss in Boots)

Sweet Tooth (Christmas – Hansel and Gretel)

Jacked Up (D/s – Jack and the Beanstalk)

Rise and Shine (Novella – Sleeping Beauty)

———

BY HJ WELCH

Paddle Creek Daddies (Small town and kink)

#1 Heaven Sent

#2 Yes, Sir

#3 Little Pleasures

#4 Four Play

#5 Hell's Kitten

#6 Make Believe

Pine Cove (Small town)

Complete Box Set

Homecoming Hearts (Former Boy Band)

Complete Box Set

Seasonal Daddies (International romance, multi-author shared universe)

Jalen & Colby: A Daddy for Christmas

Arlo: A Daddy for Summer

Bears-4-**U** (Daddies and bears, multi-author shared universe)

Keep Me

CHAPTER
One

I doubt it'll make me terribly interesting at parties, but I've become absolutely fascinated by the London Underground.

For instance, did you know that Angel station on the Northern line has the longest escalator? A whopping sixty metres! Speaking of escalators, Earl's Court was the first station to have one installed, all the way back in 1911. London's underground is actually the oldest in the whole world, opening in 1863 with the Metropolitan line and Baker Street station.

See? I'm going to be a hit with all the hot guys at parties.

I sigh and wonder when the doors on this particular tube are going to close. We're being held to regulate the service at Green Park, which used to be called Dover Street until it was changed in 1933. I bet nobody else on this entire train knows that.

Probably because they have healthy, varied social lives.

I remind myself that it's okay. I've only been living in London for a couple of weeks, for crying out loud. I grew up in a sleepy little town in Oxfordshire that I returned to after my stint at uni where I studied computer science. Living with my parents certainly helped me save money whilst in my first job, but city life had been calling to me for quite some time. I'll start my new position on Monday morning and start making friends in no time.

Hopefully. Maybe.

In the meantime, I've decided that the Jubilee line is my favourite tube line, and having a favourite tube line has got to go some way to making me a proper Londoner, surely? I like it because it feels new but not too flashy, and it's the only line connected to all the other ones on the network. Plus, it's closest to my home, so I'm probably biased, but I think that's okay. I'm sure most people prefer the line they live on.

I fidget in my seat and look around at the tired commuters and people on their way out for Friday night fun. We're on the cusp of fancy Mayfair. If I went above ground right now, I'd find myself at the Ritz. I imagine most people looking for a good time on the cheaper side would be heading in the opposite direction into central. But that's the thing about London. You can probably find somewhere for a party in any direction if you look hard enough.

I'm wrenched from my absent musings as the young man sitting next to me suddenly jerks quite violently. I hadn't realised he'd been asleep, but I assume so now from the way he frantically wipes his face and looks around. I see him clock the name of the station we're being held at.

"Shit!" he cries and bolts for the open door, pushing people aside to make his escape. He obviously missed the announcements saying we weren't going anywhere right now, and I feel a little pang of sympathy for him and his panic.

Several people glance at his now vacant seat, as do I out of habit. I generally only carry my phone, but seeing as the fold-over case also contains my debit card, driving licence, and house key, I'm fully aware of how shafted I'd be if I ever left it behind. Therefore, doublechecking it's not slipped out of my pocket is second nature.

So I immediately spy something glinting in the artificial light of the tube.

I snatch it up and discover it's a gold pocket watch. Not some cheap cosplay item ordered online, either. It's heavy in my palm and has a worn engraving on the back that makes me think it has to be some sort of family heirloom.

The doors start to beep, indicating they're about to close and we'll shortly be on the move.

Without hesitating, I lurch for the exit, people thankfully scattering as I do. Perhaps they saw me pick up the watch and correctly assumed I'm going to do my utmost to return it to its rightful owner.

"Good luck, mate!" a bloke calls out after me, and he and his friends all raise their beer cans and cheer me on.

Another fun fact: drinking on the underground became illegal in 2008. But that doesn't stop a lot of Londoners as far as I can make out.

I dive through the doors just as they close, turning to give the men a thumbs up as the train starts to pull away. *Phew.* My heart is racing from the adrenaline spike, but my little mission has only just begun.

Before I move, I check I do indeed have my phone and everything else attached to it still on my person. That would have been rather ironic, otherwise. But it's safely in my jeans pocket, where it belongs, so I quickly look around for my quarry.

He seemed to be about my age—mid-twenties—with pale skin, a slim build, and a shock of bleached white-blond hair. Not like mine, which is classified as dirty blond, something that's always made me a bit sad. Why dirty and not dark?

Anyway, back to my stranger. It's his hair more than

anything that helps me spy him just as he pushes his way through the crowd around the corner of one of the platform's exits. I sprint after him, keeping my eyes peeled for flashes of snow white amidst the other travellers.

"Excuse me! Hello!" I try calling out, earning more than a few funny looks from passersby. But Mr Pocket Watch is too far away. He might even have earbuds in, so he'd be even less likely to hear me. And how would he be aware that I meant him anyway without me knowing his name? I consider hollering 'You with the blond hair!' but not only would that be uncouth, I'm also sure the dozen or so other blonds in the vicinity wouldn't appreciate the catcalling.

So I continue my chase, relieved as I spy him turn down another corridor. I realise as I see more of his attire that he's not just wearing a suit—hardly unusual on a weekday in the city—but it's actually a tailcoat with a waistcoat and everything. The kind of posh getup you'd wear for a wedding. The pocket watch makes a little more sense now. Maybe he's heading to an evening ceremony right now, and that's why he's in such a hurry?

Whatever he's running towards, it doesn't really matter to me. I only care about reuniting him with his timepiece and then getting back on the tube so I can...

Do what, exactly? Go home to my small, one-bed flat above a newsagents in Wembley? Watch some Netflix with microwave noodles for dinner? If I stop to think about it, chasing a stranger through the bowels of the London Underground network is the most exciting thing that's happened to me since I moved here.

Of course I don't stop to think about it. I actually pick up my pace, worrying the next time I won't be there quick enough to see which way he goes.

The crowd is thinning as most people are heading up to the exit. But Mr Pocket Watch takes another corner down a smaller passageway that says it leads to an elevator. Oh, thank goodness. Hopefully, he'll have to stop and wait for the lift to arrive, and I'll be able to catch up and give him back his treasure. I'm almost sad that my little adventure was so short lived, but all that really matters is that he gets his property returned.

Except when I round the corner, he's not waiting for the elevator. A large, ornate gold key flashes in his hand as he opens what looks to me like a maintenance door.

"Excuse me!" I shout again, raising my hand to wave at him as I smile in what I hope is a friendly manner.

Apparently not.

He looks at me with wide eyes behind oval, frameless glasses that I hadn't even spotted until now. Letting out a squeak, he flinches and dashes into the cupboard.

"Hang on!" I try and stop him as I dash forwards, catching the door before it closes. I don't know where he thinks he can hide from me in there. "I just wanted to…"

Ah.

I can see why I thought he could hide. Because on the other side of the door isn't a cupboard at all. There are no mops and buckets. Nor are there any electrical boards. Certainly not a timid, bespectacled blond.

What there is, is a spiral staircase leading downwards.

I look at the door I'm still holding onto. I presume he thought it would swing shut and lock behind him so I wouldn't be able to follow. Lucky for both of us I'm nimble when I want to be. I go to take the first step down

Then stop.

He looked scared when he realised I'd seen him, which probably means he shouldn't be going down here. Which means *I* shouldn't be going down here. Getting arrested really isn't how I want to spend my weekend, especially not before I start my first London job.

I turn the watch over in my hand, trailing the chain between my fingers and looking at the engraving properly. *Tempus fugit,* it reads in swirly old-fashioned script. I'm pretty sure that's Latin. *Time flies.* I sigh and look at the gloomy stairwell with its peeling paint as a breeze hits me. Not unusual underground, with all the trains moving the air around constantly. However, I can't help but feel like I'm being called onwards. Beckoned, even.

Biting my lip, I look at the watch. If I had something precious like this, I'd be devastated to lose it simply because it slipped out of my pocket on the Jubilee line. I could always turn it in to lost and found, but…

But what's the point of moving to the big city if I just hide away from it? If I hand the watch off to someone else, I'll never know if the fancy, fussy white-haired man ever got it back. If I could put it in his hands myself, if I could see the relief on his face…well, I'd sleep better tonight, I'm sure.

Taking a deep breath, I take that first step downwards after all, allowing the door to swing shut behind me.

Who knows what lies at the bottom of these stairs? One way or another, I guess I'm about to find out.

CHAPTER
Two

Slightly gruesome fact: both Aldgate and Liverpool Street stations are built on top of plague pits dating back to the 1600s. I try not to think about that as I traverse the narrow spiral staircase, feeling pretty certain there aren't any records of mass graves in this part of west London. Although I do have to shoo away more than one vivid premonition of the end of the steps spitting me out into catacombs filled with bones like those found in Paris.

It feels like I descend forever, but it's probably only a few minutes. When I push through another door, there are no skeletons in sight, thank goodness. It's just another corridor with a curved ceiling. However, this one looks a little worse for wear.

The multitude of tunnels in the underground system are very well illuminated, but here there's only emergency lighting in the form of sporadic yellowy naked bulbs. Straining my ears, I can hear…something. After several steps closer to the sound, I realise what it is.

A bass line. Music.

My heart rate picks up. I still have no idea what I'm

walking towards, but usually, music means fun, right? It's probably not a supervillain board meeting if they're playing the latest pop hits.

Figuring that's probably where Mr Pocket Watch went, I follow the beat down the corridor, my skin tingling as it gets louder as I go. The air is surprisingly fresh. Like I said, from what I know and have experienced so far, there's always a good breeze going through the tube network no matter what station you're in. But this place does have a dilapidated, forgotten aesthetic, so it wouldn't have been so strange if it had been musty.

I look around, my footsteps my only company. On the wall, there are faded, dogeared posters calling for people to make do and mend, to keep calm and carry on, and to dig for victory.

A lump catches in my throat as the realisation dawns on me that they're from the Second World War. Tube stations were often used as air raid shelters back then. In fact, part of the Piccadilly line—which also runs through Green Park— was used to store treasures from the British Museum to keep them safe during the Blitz. This station obviously never got updated like most of the stations have been, though.

A recently read fact surfaces in my mind, as I think about where we are geographically. "Down Street," I say with a chuckle, looking around again in awe. Sure enough, farther along the corridor, those two words are spelled into the tiles. This is one of many abandoned tube stations along the network. Apparently, Winston Churchill himself used to bunker down here.

And now here I am.

I'd love to inspect every inch of this historic place, but I have someone to find. Feeling like I'm travelling back in time, I hurry along the corridor where the lights are getting dimmer and the music is getting louder. Soon all thoughts of the war fade from my mind as I round a corner and find myself on the edge of the most wondrous sight.

The base line is throbbing loudly through my bones now as techno music fills the air. Gone are the warm emergency bulbs, replaced by neon-coloured lasers cutting through the darkness. The space is filled with people in all manner of dress, from jeans like me to ballgowns, leather harnesses to pyjamas, sequins to lace that barely covers anything at all.

What have to be fake plants cover the walls of what feels like a warren of interconnected, doorless rooms. I've read about how plenty of 'under the arches' spaces have been reclaimed by bars and other businesses, but this is my first time seeing something like it. Tendrils of leaves and flowers hang from the ceiling, and the people milling about occasionally reach up to touch them absently. I can understand why. The effect is beautiful.

I can only see so far into the strange maze, but within my line of sight, there are several large bird cages on plinths so the people inside are raised above the throng of partygoers. What little clothing these dancers are wearing suggests various different animals as they writhe and undulate their shimmering bodies. I swallow, my skin tingling again. It's all rather *sexy*.

Nestled amidst the faux flora are playing cards, as if they were growing there. I also see a couple of varying sized clocks, but none of them are telling the same time, let alone the *right* time. In fact, I think some of them might even be going backwards. I frown and wonder at their purpose.

"How curious," I mutter to myself.

I've not been clubbing much, but this looks better than your average bar in Leicester Square. If I'm going to have a hope of finding my new blond friend, I'm going to have to start searching through all these nooks and crannies. So I put the watch in my own pocket for safekeeping and take a deep breath, stepping forwards to where the shabby concrete floor gives way to bright green artificial grass.

Seemingly out of nowhere, my way is suddenly blocked by two muscular chests, their owners' arms crossed in front of them. I jump backwards and look up to see identical scowling faces glaring down at me. Literally. The men look so alike they have to be twins.

"Oh, s-sorry," I stammer as I get my footing again. "I'm just…there was this young man, and he lost his watch, and…I just…well, I was trying to, um…"

I'm ashamed to say I wilt under their gaze. But with a trembling hand, I still manage to pull said watch from my pocket to show them, as if that might somehow convince them to stop glaring at me like I just insulted their mother.

"See? He's got white-blond hair. I'm sure he came this way, but…"

"Token," the one on the left grunts.

Good lord, they look like they simply live in the gym. Their bulging muscles gleam in the disco lights, making me feel like they'd been oiled up for the effect. Their black leather hotpants cling to their hips, showing off thighs that could probably crush my head like a melon. Polished black boots adorn their feet, again looking like something they could use to stomp my skull into pieces.

I try not to tremble too much. "I, um, beg your pardon?"

"Token," the one on the right repeats.

"I don't understand," I say meekly.

The left twin narrows his eyes at me, probably trying to decide if I'm taking the piss or not. "No token, no entry," he elaborates.

"Right," I utter, trying not to feel defeated. "But you see, I don't actually want to go to your party. Not that it doesn't look like a perfectly wonderful affair! I'm just trying to return this watch, and I'm certain its owner could only have come this way."

The twins remain stony-faced.

"No token," the one on the right begins to say, "no—"

"He's with me!" a voice cries from behind.

Confused, I turn around. Whoever it is must be mistaken, as I certainly didn't come down here with anyone.

But any protest I might have uttered dies on my lips as I come face to face with one of the most beautiful men I've ever seen in my life. He grins at me, his smile breathtaking.

Oh, yes.

I'm ashamed to say that I'd probably go anywhere with this handsome stranger, the consequences be damned.

I'M SURE MY MOUTH IS HANGING OPEN AS THE STRANGER JOGS towards me down the corridor, forgotten by time. He's wearing dark purple trousers made of some sort of metallic fabric that clings to his thighs and flares out around his ankles over black heeled boots. A black mesh top does little to conceal his sculpted torso or the acres of light brown skin, the threads glimmering in the dim emergency lights.

What really captures the majority of my attention, aside from his dazzling smile, is the thick, fluffy, jade-coloured tail secured to the back of his trousers and the matching pair of green fluffy cat ears emerging from his mop of thick black hair. His almond eyes sparkle as he nears, winking at me once he stops.

Goodness. Did he come from the tube dressed like that? I wonder how many broken hearts he left in his wake if he did.

I realise then that he's brandishing a gold key, just like the one Mr Pocket Watch used to get through the door in the station. Apparently, that was the token the scary-looking twins were after in order to gain entrance.

"He's with me," the stunning stranger repeats as he loops

his arm through mine. I feel my eyebrows shoot up in surprise, but he's busy grinning at the two men before us.

I clear my throat and also turn my attention back their way, giving a slight nod. If it's going to get me past these goons, I'll go along with his rouse. Although why he'd be helping me, I have no idea. I just consider myself lucky and try not to look shifty.

The twins glance at each other, seemingly deciding on whether or not one key will admit two. I have no idea if this event has a plus-one policy or not. But eventually, they turn back towards us with a grunt and step aside.

"Cheers, gents," the stranger says with another wink as he tugs me over the threshold onto the spongey artificial grass.

"T-thank you," I splutter in awe as we continue to walk arm in arm farther into the throng.

"You're very welcome," he tells me jovially.

"No, really," I insist. "I'm actually not here to party, although it does look tremendously fun. I'm trying to return something to someone. They left it on the tube. So you're actually helping them out by helping me. But you didn't have to do that. It's not like we're friends or anything."

I clear my throat, aware that I'm rambling. But the stranger looks amused rather than annoyed. He bites his lower lip and looks at me as if I'm something delicious. A pleasant shiver runs down my spine.

"Ahh, but what is a stranger other than a friend you haven't met yet?" He lets me go and thrusts his hand forwards. "I'm Cheshire."

"Cheshire?" I repeat as I tentatively shake with him.

"Yes, like the county," he confirms. "My parents decided that growing up being tormented by other children would toughen me up." I'm so horrified by this statement that I can't do anything but gape at him. But he laughs and lets go of my hand to squeeze my shoulder through my T-shirt. "I'm joking. But yes, I'm aware it's an unusual name."

"No, sorry," I say, my cheeks heating up. "I didn't mean to imply anything. I just wanted to make sure I heard you correctly." The last thing I want is for this gorgeous man to think I'm rude.

Cheshire laughs and slips his arm through mine again. "Honestly, it's fine. Don't worry. And you?"

"Me?"

He leans in to whisper conspiratorially into my ear. "Do you have a name?"

"Oh!" I cry in embarrassment. "Of course I do. Everyone does. I mean…"

Well, I'm making an absolute mess of this, aren't I? So much for playing it cool in front of someone who effortlessly oozes sex appeal.

"Alexander," I manage to utter without humiliating myself further. I'm sure any second now he's going to untangle himself from me to go find someone less dorky than me, which will probably be anyone at all.

"Alexander," he repeats in delight. "Or Alex?"

I open my mouth to confirm that yes, I always go by my full name. But something stops me.

I can be anyone I like here. I can be someone fun and exciting. Why not try on a new name for the night?

"Alex," I agree with a shy smile.

"Wonderful, Alex!" Cheshire declares, swinging his arm out to indicate the revelry. "Is this your first time joining us down here?"

I nod as he pulls me through tunnels packed with people. Deep alcoves hint at different activities going on, like mini golf, a life drawing session, and a throng around a roulette wheel. Everywhere, people are dancing, bodies writhing in the shadows as beams of colourful lights slice through, highlighting the debauchery.

Some people are doing more than dancing.

"Oh, goodness," I squeak, averting my eyes, not sure if the intention is to look or not.

"Everything okay?" Cheshire asks.

"Um-hm," I squeak, casting my thoughts around for a change in topic. I think I might die if he notices how flustered I am seeing people being naughty in the shadows.

Of course, only one topic comes to mind.

"Did you know that over fifty percent of the underground is, in fact, above ground?"

Cheshire's eyes widen at me, and I'm sure this is the moment he's going to find a way to politely ditch me. Instead, he reaches over and brushes a lock of hair away from my forehead. It's such an intimate act, it stuns me into stopping walking, and he does the same. "I did not actually know that fact," he says with humour in his voice.

What fact? Oh, yeah, my cringe-worthy underground trivia.

"Sorry," I rasp over the music, looking around at the bedlam. "I'm just a bit…"

"Overwhelmed?" Cheshire suggests. I nod again. He smiles warmly. "Don't worry. Everyone is their first time."

I bet he wasn't, but I keep that opinion to myself. "This is all a little mad," I admit.

Cheshire laughs again. It seems to come easily to him. "Oh, we're all mad here," he agrees with another delicious smile

Honestly, if he told me he was a model or an actor or something, I'd believe him. What I don't understand is why he's wasting his time on boring old me.

"Why *did* you help me get past those guys?" I ask him, hoping it's not too much of a conversation segue.

He shrugs. "You made it all the way down here. It seemed a shame to send you packing before you got to have any fun."

So that's it. He would have been kind to anyone. The realisation makes me like him even more, but it also proves that I'm not special. I was just in the right place at the right time. Except...

Why is he still by my side?

I'm pulled from my thoughts as I spy one of the better-lit alcoves. Even from this distance and all the people in between, I can see it looks like a refreshments table.

"Thirsty?" Cheshire asks.

"Yeah," I admit. I have been chasing after Mr Pocket Watch. Oh...I'm not exactly doing my best to find him anymore, am I? But...well, hopefully, he's going to be down here for a while, so that gives me some time. Surely, a quick detour won't hurt. It is dinner time, after all, and I am hungry.

The alcove is understandably busy with other people also seeking food and drink. "I don't see any prices," I say to Cheshire over the din as bodies jostle around us.

He leans into me so close his lips practically brush my ear, and I have to repress another shiver. "It's all free, little one. Well, except the gambling. That's how they make their money. But refreshments are on the house."

It takes me a second to register the pet name. *Little one.* I blink as it does very strange things to my insides. But Cheshire is already saying hello to other people and reaching for some iced sugar cookies shaped like playing cards. That seems to be a recurring theme down here. Everyone is helping themselves, and no one is paying. In fact, there's no one to give any money to anyway. But there are lots of little signs on sticks that say, 'Eat Me!' and 'Drink Me!'

I take a deep breath. Why not? Yes, I came down here

with a purpose. But what's the harm in having a little fun along the way?

There are all kinds of cake stands and bowls displaying yummy-looking goodies. But I'm drawn to the rack of test tubes filled with emerald-green liquid. Before I can talk myself out of it, I slide one free and knock it back.

Just as Cheshire looks my way, his eyes widening in alarm as he reaches for me.

"Alex!"

The drink burns the second it hits my tongue. If I had any sense, I might have spat it out. But that would be extremely rude, so I don't fight the instinct to swallow the wretched stuff as quickly as possible. Tears burn my eyes as I cough and splutter.

"Oh, Alex," Cheshire says fondly, once more by my side, already rubbing my back and holding my free hand. "I wondered if you realised that was absinthe. Have you had it before?"

I shake my head, still coughing, fretting that I might be about to sick the vile liquid right back up again. He pulls me around the overflowing table of delights, using a ladle to pour me a glass of something pink.

"Have a little lemonade to wash it down," he says, swapping the empty test tube for a full tumbler. "And take some cookies whilst you're at it. The less empty your stomach is with that poison, the better."

I hum in agreement between a gulp of refreshing pink lemonade and nibbling on a super sweet biscuit. "Thank you," I croak, feeling embarrassed. If it wasn't obvious before that I'm an innocent newbie, it is now. Perhaps his 'little one' moniker isn't so far off.

"Just take it easy," he says with his signature wink.

I nod, about to assure him that I intend to, when a flash of white-blond hair out in the main tunnel grabs my attention.

"Oh! It's him!" I turn excitedly towards Cheshire. "Mr Pocket Watch! Um, I mean, the man who lost his pocket watch on the tube."

"What are you waiting for, then?" Cheshire cries. "Go chase him!" He slaps my bottom, making me squeak in shock. Then disappointment creeps in, but that's silly. Of course he doesn't want to come with me. It's my mission, not his. He came here to party.

"Well, um, maybe see you later?"

I sound pathetic to my own ears. I've never met anyone so enigmatic as Cheshire before in my life. I really don't want to leave him because I have no doubt that as soon as I do, he'll find someone far more interesting to play with.

But I have a duty to perform, and I'll never forgive myself if I slack off and fail to return the pocket watch, especially now I know that my blond friend is without a doubt at the event.

I expect Cheshire to shrug off my departure and quickly forget all about me. Instead, he leans in and brushes his lips against my cheek in what I almost believe is a kiss. "See you later," he murmurs over the throbbing music.

My heart leaps into my throat, hope floating through me that he really means it. But I can't dither any longer and lose Mr Pocket Watch again. So I push my way back into the crowd, Cheshire's brilliant smile the last thing I see of him.

For now.

Four

Bodies swirl around me as the music pulses. I feel like I'm being carried on a turbulent tide as I move back into the more central area of the underground warren. I frantically look for the white-blond hair, but I realise that my unaware target has made life easier for me.

He's now sporting a pair of fluffy white rabbit ears.

They're not as nice as Cheshire's jade cat ears, *of course*. But they are still quite charming. One of them is folded over to make them extra cute. They certainly make it easier to pursue him through the horde of partygoers, but I'm still struggling.

"Excuse me, sorry, pardon me…"

I'm trying my best to weave around people, but that doesn't stop me from bumping into a broad-chested man in a puffy green jacket, smoking a vape.

"I'm so sorry," I apologise, trying to move around him. But he moves to block me, blinking slowly as he exhales a strawberry-scented cloud in my face, making me cough.

"Who…are…you?" he asks slowly, clearly intoxicated with

something. He's wearing fluffy green boppers on his head that jiggle as he turns his face this way and that, studying me.

I'm tempted to shove past him, but I do still have my manners. "I'm Alex," I say, getting a thrill from using my new shortened name again. I wonder if Alex is who I'll be when I get back outside. Is that my London name now? It could be. I'll be introducing myself to all kinds of people soon enough. I can use whatever name I want.

Mr Boppers hums and nods his head, causing a flurry of movement from the balls attached on springs to his head-band. Then he reaches into his puffy jacket and withdraws a brown paper bag with the edges turned down.

"Can I…*tempt* you?" he asks in that same slow, dreamy voice. Peering inside, I can see that inside the bag are mushrooms. I'm not so naïve that I don't realise exactly what kind of mushrooms they are.

"Oh, um, no thank you," I say as kindly as I can, gently pushing them back towards him. "You enjoy them."

He hums again before turning away and drifting into the throng of dancing bodies.

Sighing, I look around, but I already know I've lost Mr Pocket Watch. My first instinct is to spin around and go right back to Cheshire. I really don't want our brief encounter to be it for the night.

But…that wouldn't be very honourable. I know the white-blond hair and bunny ears were travelling this way, so I need to at least try and hunt for the watch's owner in this direction. I can try and find Cheshire again later. In fact, he invited me to do just that.

Feeling more determined, I walk on. The space opens up into more of an auditorium-like space. The ceiling is slightly higher here, enough to allow several mirror balls to be suspended above the partygoers as well as a fabulous chandelier in the centre.

At the back, there's a slightly raised stage against one of the walls with an ornate but empty throne standing in the centre. It feels like it's waiting for someone to come fill it.

Whilst there seems to be dancing in every corner of this place, this area is bigger than the other tunnels and there looks to be a specific light-up floor dedicated to boogying here. There are also more animal performers dotted around in cages on plinths. In addition, I see someone juggling, another swinging poi around in circles, and a fire-breather that makes me jump as she blows out a flame like a dragon.

As I fumble my way through the crowd, looking for any sign of white rabbit ears, I stumble upon what I immediately realise is a chess game. The board is on the floor, nestled in the artificial grass, and the pieces are actually people dressed in either white or red to represent the different sides.

'Dressed' might be too generous a term. These people—masculine, feminine, and in between—are scantily draped with gauzy materials that leave almost nothing to the imagination. When I blink and look at the already discarded pieces, I can see why. It seems the object of the game is to get out as soon as possible, shed your clothes into a red or white pile, and then—*ahem*—get busy.

I was already pretty well aware that people were having sex at this party, but I've never seen actual orgies before outside of porn. In fact, not much in porn even so. I guess I'm quite a timid, vanilla little one, just like Cheshire thought.

I wonder if I still will be after I make it through tonight.

Perhaps I need a drink to fortify myself. No more absinthe, thank you very much. But I do see another bar in a different alcove, this one with a bartender. The idea of a fruity cocktail sounds fun, so I make my way over. Hopefully, Mr Pocket Watch hasn't gone too far. Although, if my experience has taught me anything so far tonight, it's that he's sure to pop up again soon enough.

Quite a gaggle is waiting to be served, but I patiently wait my turn. I split my time between looking around for Mr Pocket Watch and studying the bar setup. A large mirror is hung up on the back wall behind the various bottles of liquor and the people serving it. There's a word painted onto it, but it takes me a moment to realise that not only is the word spelled backwards, but the letters are, too. It's a mirror image. E-R-A-W-E-B. Beware.

I chuckle, thinking how that's probably an apt warning for this place.

There are, in fact, three people serving drinks here. One has mouse ears, another brown rabbit ears a bit like Mr Pocket Watch, and the one who seems to be in charge has a black top hat and a tailcoat, again like my new blond friend. Other than that, the cute twinks are wearing nothing but hot pants in various colours, like the twin bouncers out front. I wonder if it's a sort of company uniform, and gulp at the prospect of sporting anything like that myself.

I also consider the frantic bartenders. They suit the label 'twink' in their skimpy outfits with glitter all over them. I've often thought about if I count as a twink. Sadly, I don't think I'm fabulous enough. Just sort of small, quiet, and boring.

Yet again, I ponder why Cheshire wanted to spend any time with me at all, let alone sneak me into this event as his plus-one. Does he really want to see me again? I know I want to see him.

If I'm going to be less quiet and boring, I probably need to make a conscious effort to do so. I take a deep breath and nod to myself. I'm going to have this drink, find Mr Pocket Watch, then find my new friend with the gorgeous smile.

This time I won't let him go so easily.

"Next, please!" the server with the top hat cries. He's got a slip of paper in his hatband that says 10/6. I don't know if that's supposed to be a fraction or a date or something else entirely.

I find myself jostled in front of him. I guess I'm next. It was nice of people not to push in front of me. But as I look at the drinks menu, I let out a sort of pained groan. I've never heard of any of these things in my life. What the devil is a Bandersnatch? A Mome Rath? A Vorpal Blade?

"Come along, come along!" the bartender cries, making me panic. "If you don't kill time, it'll kill you!"

What nonsense. But Mr Top Hat is laughing and dancing around in front of me, which softens my irritation. It's not his fault I decided to get a drink when I should be looking for not just one but two people, and now I don't know what to order.

"Um, are any of those cocktails sweet?" I ask.

"How about a Jubjub Bird?" he suggests, spinning around as his mouse friend rushes past him on his way to make another patron a drink.

"Sounds great," I say in relief. Honestly, I'll take anything that isn't absinthe and that will take the edge of my nerves.

What I'm presented with is a blue connection in a floral china teacup resting on a matching saucer. Mr Top Hat raises his eyebrows as he hands it to me, and I interpret that as wanting me to take a sip to see if I like it.

"Ohh," I say as soon as I swallow. "That's delicious!"

Mr Top Hat bows with a flourish of his hand. "And a very happy birthday to you indeed, good sir!"

"Oh, it's not my…" I trail off when I realise he's already flitted off to serve the next person. Perhaps he wishes everyone a happy birthday once they have their drink? It's silly, but I also think it's kind of nice.

I happily push my way back from the bar so others can be served. The cocktail really is yummy, tasting sweet but also a little sour, just enough to give it a tang. It has to have a couple of different kinds of alcohol mixed in under the fruity syrup flavours, as I can already feel the effects hitting my bloodstream.

Good. This place might be strange, but if I can stop worrying so much, I might enjoy it more. I could also have better luck finding my quarry if I'm more relaxed.

I stand to one side, sipping from my cup, my eyes drifting over the frivolities. And then it's like the room takes a breath, people parting ever so slightly, and there he is again.

Cheshire.

He's dancing by himself on the light-up floor, looking perfectly at ease. His hips are so sexy as they sway to the beat, his green tail swishing behind him like it's actually alive. His arms are raised in the air like he doesn't have a care in the world. I can't help but stare.

Then he opens his eyes and looks directly at me. I gulp. He crooks a finger, enticing me back to him.

He really doesn't have to try very hard.

CHAPTER
Five

I DON'T HESITATE TO NECK THE REST OF MY BLUE DRINK AND set the cup and saucer down on a nearby table. My heart hammers in my chest as I weave past people to reach Cheshire, who hasn't taken his eyes off me.

"Hi," I say breathlessly as I reach him. It still doesn't quite seem real that he's interested in me in any way. His gaze blazes across my skin as he looks me up and down, though, and I can't help but shiver under his attention.

"Hi," he replies smoothly over the pounding music. "Did you find who you were looking for?"

"No," I say, shame creeping back into my chest. "I keep losing him."

"It is packed in here," Cheshire says sympathetically.

His body is still swaying to the rhythm, and he looks so effortlessly cool. I'm sure I look as awkward as anything, but I try and move with him. The alcohol has helped a little with my inhibitions, at least.

"Do you want to keep looking?" he asks.

I know I should, but I can't bear to tear myself away from this moment. "Maybe in a minute?" I shout over the din.

Cheshire rewards me with one of his breathtaking smiles. "I doubt he'll be going far," he assures me. When he touches his hand to my hip, my breath hitches, my skin feeling electrified.

"If you spy anyone with white rabbit ears, let me know," I say with a laugh. If I keep up the pretence that we're sort of looking around, I'll feel less guilty.

"Bunny Boy?" Cheshire asks, his eyebrows jumping up. "Bleached-blond hair to match those ears?"

"Yes!" I cry incredulously. "How did you know?"

He laughs. "Oh, everyone knows him. He's part of the court."

"The court?" I repeat.

Cheshire nods. "In fact…" He looks towards the stage and points. "Here we go!"

The music changes, as do the lights. A cheer goes through the crowd as a drag queen takes to the stage. My jaw drops at her outrageously gorgeous dress that looks like something straight out of a Regency ball. Voluminous skirts, puffy sleeves, and a plunging neckline make it all very dramatic. Not to mention that colour scheme of red, white and black, accentuated by her audacious gold jewellery, including a crown with heart-shaped red jewels seated in her ridiculously high hair. The top of the wig almost touches the fake foliage on the ceiling as she takes her place on the throne that I noted earlier, looking like it was waiting for someone to occupy it.

"Who's that?" I ask in awe.

"Miss Royal Flush," Cheshire informs me. He's standing behind me now as we both watch the stage. It doesn't look like the queen is going to entertain us. Rather, she's watching all the other performers on their various plinths. I feel Cheshire's warm breath against my neck as his words tickle my ear. "She's the mother of the Haus of Cards. This is their gig, their shindig."

"What, the party?" I ask, glancing over my shoulder to look at him.

Cheshire tilts his head from side to side. "It's kind of more of a lifestyle. But, yeah. They run all of this."

"They pay for it?" I ask incredulously.

I never want to judge anyone, but I always got the impression that drag queens didn't make a lot of money unless they'd been on the telly, and even then, a lot of them aren't *rich* rich. Aside from making money from the roulette table and other games Cheshire mentioned, I did wonder how they could afford not to be charging for food and drink. My assumption was they were being backed by someone with real money.

Cheshire gives me one of his winks that I'm coming to adore. "The rumour is Miss Royal might be some kind of *actual* minor royalty."

"Oh," I say, my voice fluttering as I look around again.

It's not as if I've exactly felt *in* my depth since I arrived here, but I certainly feel even more out of it at this point. Who are all these people? What kind of event have I crashed? Is being arrested still on the cards?

I look at Royal Flush as she observes the scene. It looks like there's a special dance being performed just for her. I can't tell from her scowling face if she's impressed or appalled.

"Is she always so…"

"Terrifying?" Cheshire supplies with a chuckle. "Pretty much. I'd just stay out of her way. It's the simplest path to an easy life."

Craning my neck, I can see a couple of other people lounging in a pile of cushions on the stage near the queen. They're so beautifully dressed I imagine them to almost be like living dolls, not there to enjoy the revelries but to be ornaments for Miss Royal's viewing pleasure.

There's a super hot guy with a square jaw, wearing tailored trousers and a Venetian mask. What's visible behind it shows piercing eyes. He might have a six-pack, but he doesn't exactly look friendly. Then there's a flat-chested woman in lacy lingerie, knee-high boots, full-length gloves, and glittery butterflies in her exquisitely styled hair. She's at least smiling demurely and waving to people in the crowd. A few more people are leaning on the stage, all looking like they're about to do some sort of runway at London Fashion Week.

I glance down at my jeans and T-shirt. They're not exactly shabby. I wore them out when I was doing a little sightseeing today, after all. But if I'd known I was coming here tonight, I might have at least put on a button-down or something.

Rather than fret about my appearance, I remind myself that Cheshire doesn't seem to mind what I'm wearing, as he's still dancing with me. So I clear my throat and recall why we were talking about the court in the first place.

"So Mr Pocket Watch…Bunny Boy…he's with her? Miss Royal?" If that's the case, no wonder he's looked stressed since I first laid eyes on him. She seems intense.

Cheshire hums and wraps his arms around me, swaying us in time to the music. I try not to gasp too much in case he feels it, but I can't help it. This gorgeous guy is dancing with me, hugging me, spending all this time with me.

It feels almost like I've slipped into a dream.

"Yeah, he's part of the Haus of Cards, so he'll definitely be here all night."

"That's good," I say with genuine relief. I've got a little bit of grace and don't have to worry so much that I'm not spending every minute searching for him.

Although…

I glance back at Cheshire and remind myself that tonight I'm Alex, a braver version of Alexander. Alex can take a chance. He can ask for what he wants…what he *desires.* Because what's the worst that can happen? Yeah, this handsome stranger could turn me down, but then what? I'll probably never see him again. Why not be outrageous?

"I would still like to find him sooner rather than later," I admit. "Would you, um, maybe help me look?"

Naturally, I expect him to scoff and go and finally find someone more fun to hang around with. But his face lights up like I've just made his whole night. "I'd love to, little one!"

"Really?" As happy as I am, I'm also a bit surprised. "Are you sure you don't want to carry on dancing and drinking and…well…" I blush. Whatever else he usually does at these sorts of parties.

He gives me a one-armed shrug and a lazy grin. "The quicker we find Mr Rabbit, the quicker we can get back to doing all those things together."

Together.

My heart somersaults in my chest. I must confess, that was exactly my motivation as well. If I don't have to fret about the pocket watch anymore, I can give Cheshire all my attention. Nothing like this has ever happened to me before. I'm not the kind of guy whom hot, confident men notice. I don't want to waste any more of my night on my mission than I can help.

I gulp and smile back at him. "Sounds like a plan."

He nuzzles his nose against my cheek, so close to being a kiss my heart almost stops entirely. But he pulls away before I can lose consciousness, leaning in to whisper against my ear again.

"I know just the place to start looking. Come on."

Like I thought when I very first saw him: That's a no-brainer. I'll go anywhere he asks me to.

Six

When Cheshire slips his hand against mine, I feel so elated I could float away. Good job he squeezes it tight, tethering me to the ground.

He pulls me along, weaving through the throng until we break free of the dance floor, our feet once more on the artificial grass. Instead of going back the way we came, he tugs me farther down the tunnel, passing by more alcoves filled with interesting activities. Amongst other things, I see a poetry reading being performed by a man dressed as a walrus to listeners at an oyster bar.

Wild.

The archway we stop at has a curtain of flowered tendrils covering the entrance. My heart rate picks up as he gently pushes them aside to lead us into a darkened space.

Immediately, I notice that the music is muffled for the first time all evening. In here, the speakers are playing something else much more chilled, like ambient sound you'd hear at a spa or maybe at a poolside lounge. It's just enough to overpower the DJ booth back in the main area that's pumping through the whole party.

It's also not an alcove but another bigger space like the one with the dance floor and the stage. There isn't just artificial grass and foliage along the walls and ceiling, but potted plants creating hedge-type separations as well. Plush cushions are scattered everywhere. The only illumination comes from the fairy lights entwined in the bushes. Fake flowers burst from every nook and cranny, making this feel like a secret garden.

Except it's not so secret. There are plenty of bodies in here also muffling the sound.

Mostly naked bodies.

There are people dancing dreamily, and some cuddled up, talking in low tones. Those still seem to generally have the most intimate parts covered. But a *lot* of people are engaged in various acts of touching and moaning and thrusting and...*oh!*

"Is this okay?" Cheshire murmurs in my ear.

I jump and gulp, spinning around to look at his mischievous face. But he's still got my hand in his, rubbing his thumb reassuringly against the backs of my knuckles. In that moment, I know that if I said I wasn't okay, he'd lead me back out into the main party area.

"Do you, um, really think the rabbit could be in here?" I say, almost managing not to squeak out the words.

"No, I don't think he's really in here," he says. His gaze flicks to my mouth, and my heart threatens to leap right out of my throat.

I do my best to swallow it back down and not tremble too much. Is he asking what I think he's asking? "Oh," I utter.

He keeps rubbing my hand soothingly. "Do you want to keep looking for him?"

"Now?" There's no escaping the squeak that time.

He gives another one-armed shrug, his easiness radiating sexiness. "Or later. It's up to you, little one."

Damn it, that makes it even worse. I don't want to make the decision! That's scary!

But…

But he's already told me he'd be all right with whatever I decide. We can walk back out again and forget this hedonistic room and just spend the rest of the night dancing. The way he's looking at me with those warm, beautiful almond eyes tells me that he'd probably be okay with that and all.

But would I?

Or would I regret it forever that I was too afraid to take a chance on what could be a truly mind-blowing, life-changing experience.

"W-we could stay here a little while, I suppose," I say without too much stuttering. "If Mr Pocket Watch is going to be around all night."

"All night," Cheshire promises, his words sounding like a purr.

He nuzzles his nose against my cheek again. However, this time he gently places a kiss against my jaw. There's no hope of me restraining my gasp now, especially not when it turns into a moan, and I grip his muscular arms to stop my weak knees from sending me crashing to the ground.

"I…oh…um…" My eyelids flutter closed as I try and form a coherent sentence, but the words aren't forthcoming.

He pulls back and caresses my cheek with his thumb. His eyes search mine. "What do you want, little one? You're in control."

I sincerely doubt that. But I feel something touch my head, and look around to see a pretty naked girl who's draped only in purple gauze. She's smiling sweetly at me as she drifts by with an armful of flower crowns in all different colours.

Reaching up, I can feel that she's given me one. When I take it off, I see it's a light blue. I can't help but love it and what I think it means. It's as if she's telling me that I'm welcome here. That I belong.

Placing it back on my head, I watch as she melts into the darkness. Then I take a deep, fortifying breath.

What am I afraid of? What's the worst that can happen? I know I've only just met him, but I trust Cheshire when he says that I'm in charge. If I change my mind, I know he'll respect that.

Everyone here is just having fun. They're lost in their own worlds. They look like they're all having a *really* great time.

I turn back to look at Cheshire and lick my lips. He asked me what I want. It's time to be brazen.

"I want you," I manage to utter.

He blesses me with the full version of that simply breathtaking smile. "I can assure you, little one, that the feeling is entirely mutual."

He firmly cups the side of my face and presses his lips against mine. It doesn't matter that we only just met. It's as if I've been waiting forever for this moment.

My heart feels like it explodes in my chest as our mouths move together, deepening the kiss. I cling to him as his tongue slips through, and mine eagerly greets it. He tastes spicey and warm and absolutely delicious.

"Come with me," he says, not knowing I already pledged to do just that from the moment I laid eyes on him.

He entwines his fingers with mine, tugging gently as we move farther inside the secret garden. I'm aware of people enjoying their pleasure all around us, but I only have eyes for the beautiful man before me. He glances back at me with a grin, and I inadvertently let out a nervous chuckle. Yes, I'm a bit anxious, as I'm not sure what exactly is about to transpire. But I'm also *excited.* I certainly never did anything like this back home or at uni. It's about time I started sowing some wild oats, right?

In a little corner behind a shrub covered in red roses and twinkling fairy lights, Cheshire finds an unoccupied, cosy-looking pile of cushions. He bites his lips as he swings me around, startling a bubbling laugh out of me. Then he gently pushes me down.

This is really happening.

It hits me all of a sudden that I absolutely can't wait.

CHAPTER
Seven

Less than ten percent of tube stations are located south of the Thames. Unlike the blood in my body, all of which is currently rushing south of *my* Thames.

Yeah, I know that doesn't make sense. There's no blood in my brain to help it function, remember?

Before I can lie all the way down, Cheshire is straddling my hips and sneaking his hands under my T-shirt. "Is this okay?" he asks, lifting it up.

My heart is racing a mile a minute, but I manage to nod. "Yeah," I croak, raising my arms. Looking delighted, he yanks the garment up and tosses it away.

I'm fully aware that he's had his chest on display through the mesh top all night, so it shouldn't freak me out to also expose myself. But he's so fit and gorgeous, and I…well, I work in IT. Unsurprisingly, I'm a little on the skinny and pale side.

But I don't get a chance to feel self-conscious. As soon as the T-shirt is discarded, Cheshire's hands are on me, running up my flanks, and he's bending down to capture one of my nipples in his mouth.

"Fuck!" I cry out in shock, making him laugh as he licks and sucks at the tender nub.

"Do you like that, Alex?"

Hearing him use my new shortened name is unreasonably erotic. It feels possessive for some reason. Maybe because he was the one who suggested it earlier? It's not like I belong to him now or anything. That would be silly.

In that moment, however, as I'm pressed against the ticklish artificial grass, my head resting on a pillow Cheshire put there for me, I certainly feel like his.

"What do you, uh, want to, um…"

With a gentle laugh, Cheshire relinquishes my nipple to kiss my mouth again, his hands already tackling the button and zip on my jeans. "I want to do whatever you want, little one," he mumbles against my lips. "And I want you naked. If that's going to be a problem, tell me now or forever hold your peace."

For a second, my brain short-circuits. It's not like I haven't had sex before, far from it. But we're in *public.* Yeah, this nook is pretty secluded, but anyone could walk in on us at any second.

Why does that excite me rather than terrify me?

In a rush of confidence, I toe my trainers off my feet and nod fervently. "I want that, too."

Cheshire hums and strips me down. I lift my hips and help him kick the jeans and underwear away. My cock is *obscene* as it springs free, bright red and leaking. Cheshire's eyes light up at the sight of it, and before I know what's happening, he dives down to take it into his mouth, wrapping his hand around the base and stroking me off.

I let out a string of profanities in as quiet a hiss as I can manage. It's not that I'm embarrassed about being overheard —because that idea is apparently ridiculously hot to me right now—I just don't want to disturb anyone else's experience by cursing like a sailor at the top of my lungs.

Squeezing my eyes shut, I grab a nearby pillow with one hand to fist it like a stress ball. The other, I slip through Cheshire's hair, loving the feel of him bobbing up and down as he worships my length with reverence. I run my thumb over one of his fluffy green ears.

I'm getting a blow job from a cat.

The thought tips me over the edge of reason, a slightly hysterical laugh escaping from my throat.

Cheshire pops off my dick looking extremely proud of himself, his lips shiny and saliva dripping from his chin that he wipes off with the back of his hand. "You like that, huh, little one?" His voice is already a bit hoarse, and the realisation that my cock did that goes straight to my balls. Which is a slight problem when he starts fondling them.

I suck in a breath. As amazing as that feels, I really don't want to blow my load just yet. The bastard knows what he's doing, though, grinning as he circles his other hand back around my shaft.

"You look stunning like this," he says, and I'm too lust-drunk to even refute it. I'm sure I blush, though, which seems to please him. "You do!" he insists. "You were stunning before, but like this, writhing and sweating...*urgh.*" He leans down, still manhandling me as he captures my lips for a filthy kiss, mumbling into my mouth, "I really want to fuck you, Alex. Can I?"

I let out a very dignified yelp. It's not like I didn't wonder if that was where this was heading. However...

"Um, yes," I say breathlessly. "I'd, um, love that. But do you...? I mean, I don't have any, um..."

He grins and reaches into the back pocket of those dark purple trousers that I've already decided deserve their own fan club. "Are you asking if I came prepared to fuck a gorgeous little treat like you, Alex?" He proudly shows me a condom packet and a sachet of lube. "Why, yes. Yes, I did."

The idea that he could be seducing someone else right now if I hadn't accidentally stumbled down here gives me a flash of jealousy, but it's only fleeting. Because I *am* here right now, watching as he unzips himself and shoves the trousers down just enough to free his thick, rock-hard cock.

There's no one else here in this secluded corner tonight. Just us. And I'm going to make the most of every single second of it.

Cheshire grabs another pillow, and I wonder what he's doing until he flips me over, and I realise it's to protect my overly sensitive member from being rubbed against the ground. The artificial grass isn't *that* soft, and I appreciate his thoughtfulness.

It's the last thing that crosses my mind before he pulls my cheeks apart and his tongue licks all the way from my balls to my crack. At that point, my brain blue-screens like an unhappy computer.

I, on the other hand, am *extremely* happy.

I'm sure the sounds I'm making are positively feral, but it's like I have no control over my body any longer. I'm just a puddle of goo as Cheshire rims me into oblivion. His tongue and fingers gradually work me open in the best kind of torture. But eventually, he withdraws, and then…

I groan pornographically as his lubed-up cock starts pressing against my entrance. I lift my hips to meet him, hugging the cushion under my head as I stick my arse wantonly in the air for him like an animal in heat.

"So good, so perfect," he's whispering as he eases farther inside me. His fingers are digging into my hips.

Is it wrong to hope they leave bruises?

"Oh, oh," I cry as he nudges against my prostate and fireworks explode in front of my closed eyes.

He's pretty much bottomed out already, so he pauses and rubs a hand up and down my spine. "How does that feel, little one?" he asks, panting slightly.

"Fucking brilliant," I slur against my pillow.

His laugh is raucous, and I peek through my eyelashes to see his head is dropped back in mirth. I feel a burst of pride that I did that to this handsome stranger. After a few more seconds, he looks back down again with a devilish grin. He starts to roll his hips, and I wonder how long it's going to take before I completely shake apart.

The last thing I see before I'm so overwhelmed I have to shut my eyes again is Cheshire's jade-green tail swishing behind him as he starts to fuck me in earnest.

My beautiful, mysterious cat man.

As much as I want this to last, there's no fighting the climax rapidly building inside me. Apparently, Cheshire feels the same. Way too soon, he snaps his hips and digs his fingers into my flesh with a bellow. I whimper and cling to my pillow as he uses me to wring every last drop of pleasure from his body.

When he finally stills, I'm trembling and breathing heavily, my cock still like steel. He eases himself out, pulls off the condom, and ties it off. As he tucks himself away in his trousers, I'm worried for a second that he's going to leave me high and dry.

But then he's gently turning me onto my back once more, fussing with the pillows so I'm all nestled in and cosy. Then he props himself up with his left hand so he can hover his body over mine, offering me up that gorgeous smile of his as he curls his fingers around my throbbing length.

"You're so pretty, Alex," he murmurs as he slowly teases me, stroking his hand up and down. I've never been called 'pretty' before, and I know it makes me blush harder as I pant. He hums and gently places kisses on my cheeks, my forehead, and even the tip of my nose. "So pretty. I'm so happy I found you tonight so you could be all mine. You're like a dream."

I'm quite sure he's got that the wrong way around, but I'm too far gone to even think about correcting him. His hand is speeding up now, flying over my cock as he kisses my lips and whispers sweet nothings to me. I whimper, a tear escaping and rolling down the side of my face.

"It's okay," he promises me. "I've got you. I'm here. Just let go and fly."

My orgasm crashes through me like waves on the shore, hitting me over and over until it finally subsides. I've covered his hand and my torso with my mess, but he doesn't seem to care. He leans down and kisses my lips softly.

"So perfect," he mumbles again.

After a minute, I manage to catch my breath and blink my eyes back into focus. Cheshire is still above me, smiling fondly.

"Hello," he says playfully.

"Hello," I say, trying not to blush anymore, if that's even possible. I don't want to ruin the moment, but… "Um…" I say, looking down at the drying cum on my skin.

He laughs and pecks another kiss on my mouth. "Yeah, let's get you cleaned up and dressed again so we can go find this pesky rabbit, hmm? Let me just…oh."

As he looks behind him, he pauses, then he glances back at me with widening eyes.

"Oh?" I repeat, concern creeping in.

"Yeah," he says with a grimace. "Uh-oh."

"What's 'uh-oh'?" I ask, my heart rate picking up again for entirely different reasons.

"Now, I don't want you to panic," Cheshire begins, naturally making me immediately want to panic, "but we seem to have a slight problem."

"Okay?" I prompt him. He winces.

"It's your clothes."

"What about them?"

He laughs nervously and rubs the back of his head. "They appear to be, well…gone."

Eight

DID YOU KNOW THAT A GRANDFATHER CLOCK WAS ONCE LEFT on the tube? A pocket watch I get. But how do you lose a whole seven-foot clock? Something like that, surely you'd keep an eye on.

You'd think so, wouldn't you?

"Gone?" I splutter in horror. "My clothes?"

As I bolt upright, Cheshire quickly scoots off me, and we both look frantically around our little corner of the secret garden.

My jeans, T-shirt, and underwear are gone. All that's left are my shoes, which I guess I should be grateful for. But that stills leaves me *totally naked in the middle of an underground party!*

"It's okay, it's okay," Cheshire assures me. He grips my shoulders tightly. "Take a deep breath."

I can't, though. I'm still frantically searching, like my missing clothing might miraculously appear. However, as I shove a cushion aside, I do catch a lucky break.

"Oh my goodness," I cry with a rush of relief. Whatever happened to my jeans, at least by some miracle, both the rabbit's pocket watch and my phone with my cards and key inside fell out. Or maybe the thief took them out? Who knows?

They must have snuck up on us when we were…well, you know. The idea of being robbed whilst I was vulnerable like that isn't quite as hot as being watched.

A lump rises in my throat as I curl my legs up, trying to at least try and cover myself up a bit. I have cum drying on my belly, for crying out loud.

"Hey, hey," Cheshire says, shaking his head and wrapping his hands around my shoulders. "It'll be okay, all right? I'm going to fix this." He glances down at himself. Perhaps he was intending to give me some of his own clothes, but he doesn't exactly have any going spare. "Right, um…wait here!"

"Where are you going?" I ask in horror.

He leans in and gives my lips a firm kiss. "Like I said. I'm going to fix this. But I'll get some friends to help you, too. Don't worry."

I'm afraid worrying is all I'm doing as he springs to his feet. Nervously, I watch as he leans around the shrub that's been shielding us. He frowns slightly until his eyebrows shoot up and he waves with a grin.

"Ladies! Can you help us out?"

He winks at me, making my heart flutter despite the circumstances. Then he dashes out of sight, leaving me all alone.

I hug my knees tighter and wonder if instead of being the greatest adventure of my life, this has actually turned into the worst disaster.

Before I can spiral too violently, a head pokes around the side of the fake rose bush. It's the cute girl who gave me my flower crown. I'd forgotten all about it, but I glance behind me, and it's there, presumably having fallen off my head when I was otherwise engaged.

For something to do, I pick it up again and fiddle with it between my hands. When I look up, the girl is beckoning to someone I can't see. She's also wearing a crown now—hers is purple. She still only has the purple gauze covering her plump frame, not leaving much of anything to the imagination. But that makes me oddly more at ease, I guess because we're in the same situation. Although she is by choice and I'm very much not, but I'll take what comfort I can get.

She comes into mine and Cheshire's little corner and kneels in front of me. She has such a kind face it makes me relax a fraction. She carefully plucks the crown from my fingers before reverently placing it back on my head with a nod.

"Thank you," I whisper. She reaches out and brushes my cheek where I guess a tear had fallen.

Behind her, several more faces peek around the bush. They're sporting different coloured flower crowns themselves. My first impression is that they're all young women, but I know better than to assume anyone's gender in a place like this. They giggle at each other before filling the small space. They're all wearing gauzy robes to match their crowns like the first girl, but it's not awkward to have so much flesh on display so close to me. It actually feels natural. Beautiful in its own way.

I don't know what Cheshire told them, but they've come armed. One cleans the mess from my belly and gives me a wet wipe so I can also take care of my more intimate area. One has a blanket to cover my modesty, even though I'm feeling less exposed amongst them now. Another lifts up my crown temporarily to brush my hair as another hands me a glass of water.

The first girl—the one I think of as *my* flower girl—has produced a pot of light blue glitter from somewhere. It's the same shade as my crown, which I suspect is on purpose as she dips a brush into the container and starts painting the gel lightly over my cheeks and the bridge of my nose, giving me glittery freckles. I chuckle at the absurdity of it but don't try and stop her, even when she does the same to my shoulders. When I put my T-shirt back on, I guess it'll stick. But the goop will come out in the wash, won't it? So why fret now?

That's *if* I get my clothes back at all. I'm not overly attached to them. It's not like they're hugely sentimental or anything. But they are mine, I paid money for them, and I would quite like them back. At the very least so I can make my way home once the night is done without getting arrested.

Apparently, that concern is a reoccurring theme this evening.

A pang makes my chest ache. What's going to happen after tonight? Will I see Cheshire again?

I probably have enough to worry about right now, so I do my best to shove those thoughts away. *One problem at a time, Alex.* I smile at all the flower girls who it seems are satisfied that I'm cleaned up and hydrated, so they're now watching as the first girl styles my hair with more glitter. Another girl applies a little extra just under my eyebrows, and another produces a lip gloss from somewhere, swiping it expertly onto my mouth.

I've never worn make-up in my life, not even for Halloween or school plays. I was always too afraid that people would laugh at me. But in that moment, I feel the way Cheshire saw me mere moments ago.

Pretty.

The girls are still fussing over me as the man himself reappears around the rose bush, looking triumphant. But when he sees me, his excited expression drops as his mouth forms a little 'o' shape.

"You look so beautiful," he murmurs. The flower girls

giggle and scoot aside as he kneels down and shows no hesitation as he presses his lips to mine. "And you taste good, too," he says cheekily.

"You came back," I say without thinking.

He scoffs. "Of course I came back," he says warmly. But then he winces. "I wasn't *entirely* successful, but I did manage to find something I think will help us out."

I realise then that he is holding something that's too small to be either my jeans or my T-shirt. Is it my briefs? That would be a bit embarrassing if so. I know we just, um, got quite close. But the idea that he might be holding the pants I was wearing all day makes me cringe.

It's a good thing that the reality is so much worse.

Before I can fret any further about my worn underwear being in his grasp, he flicks his wrist and catches the other side of the fabric, proudly displaying a tiny pair of metallic blue hotpants.

"Ta-da!"

I think I'm going to pass out.

CHAPTER
Nine

"WELL, I THINK YOU LOOK FANTASTIC," CHESHIRE DECLARES.

I bite my lower lip and turn in a circle to look down at my exposed body, like a dog trying to catch its own tail. I wish I had a mirror. I doubt very much that I look 'fantastic' as Cheshire says, but at least I might be able to check that I don't look terrible.

"I'm so naked," I whimper.

Cheshire pulls me to him, resting his hands on my hips and gently kissing my forehead. "Yes, and it's glorious. If I ever discover who took your clothes, I might have to hug them."

"You can hug them after I slap them," I grumble.

"They might enjoy that," Cheshire warns me, and I roll my eyes.

"Okay. I guess this will have to do. At least my bits and pieces are tucked away."

Cheshire grins and shakes his head. "You're adorably coy for someone who just had a public orgasm."

My now permanent blush gets hotter, but there's a hint of

pride in his words that I hold onto. He is teasing me, but I'm sure he's not being mean.

"Besides," he carries on, poking my flower crown and glancing at my feet. "You're not *just* wearing the itty-bitty hot pants that match your pretty eyes, are you?"

I sigh, deciding to simply resign myself to my fate. It's not like I'll look out of place at this party, after all. I'll just have to work out what to do when I leave, but hopefully that won't be for a while yet. Who knows? Maybe my clothes will magically reappear by then.

"Right," I say, trying to sound confident. I slip my phone into the zipped pocket at the back of the hotpants where it just about fits, then turn the watch over in my hand. "Shall we continue on our rabbit hunt?"

Cheshire presses a chaste kiss to my lips, then nods. "Sounds like a plan. Hopefully, nobody else decided to wear white ears tonight. Let's go and start scouring the crowd."

A tap on my arm makes me pause. My flower girl is looking at me with big eyes as she holds her hands up to the back of her head, mimicking rabbit ears. Not for the first time, I wonder if she and her friends have taken on some sort of vow of silence.

Or maybe flowers don't talk in the real world, so they don't down here, either.

Whatever the case, her meaning is pretty clear. "Yes, we're looking for a young man with white rabbit ears," I confirm with her.

"Bunny Boy," Cheshire elaborates.

My girl and the other flowers start pointing excitedly back out through the secret garden towards the main party area. "You saw him that way?" I ask.

They nod, and my girl moves her hands farther up her head, waggling her fingers like…

Like a crown!

"Oh!" I say excitedly, batting at Cheshire's arm as I nod at her rapidly. "Are you saying he's joined the court on stage with the queen?"

All the flower girls nod, grin, and clap happily. Cheshire smiles back at them and bows from his waist.

"As always, ladies, you have outdone yourselves. Thank you very much." He turns back to me and winks. "Would you like to join me on a stroll towards the stage area, little one?"

He holds out his arm, and I slip mine through it. Being practically naked in front of an inordinate number of strangers doesn't seem so horrifying if he's going to be by my side.

"I'd love to," I tell him.

The flower girls wave us goodbye, and we make our way back out to the main tunnel again. As soon as we push through the curtain made of vines separating the secret garden from everything else, we're hit by a wall of sound. After our brief respite of calm, it fills my chest, and the bassline makes my teeth ache. But I'm sure I'll quickly get used to it once more.

This time, it's me leading Cheshire through the packed bodies with determination. Once my duty is done, I can focus one hundred percent on him. My heart is still fluttering in my chest, as I think about what we just did together. I've never opened myself up so quickly to anyone like that in my life. I really hope it wasn't a mistake. But whether it was foolish or not, I still can't help but trust him.

The main area is pretty much just as we left it. People dancing on the light-up floor, the 'Beware' bar serving thirsty patrons, another game of human chess on the go, people in animal costumes performing in cages around the room. And at the head of it all, Miss Royal Flush with her Haus of Cards.

There are a couple of different members of the court draped over the stage now, with various others hovering nearby. But at the queen's feet sits a familiar figure. His shirt and tailcoat are gone, but he's still wearing the waistcoat with the smart trousers, frameless glasses perched on his nose and the white rabbit ears nestled in his blond hair.

My breath hitches. For the first time all night, he's not running off. *Finally!*

"Shall I just…go over there?" I ask Cheshire hesitantly. I'm not sure what protocol there is, if there is any.

He squeezes my hand. "You can do this," he tells me.

There are so many people, so I let go of Cheshire and begin navigating my way towards the stage, my eyes on the prize. I keep my hand wrapped firmly around the pocket watch. It would be a disaster to lose it now.

As I get closer, my nerves increase. But really, what do I have to be afraid of? Yes, this whole scenario is quite overwhelming, and Miss Royal Flush looks as intimidating as ever as she peers over the assembly. However, all I'm doing is returning what I'm sure is a cherished possession. Nothing to be frightened of.

Except as I near the court, I realise I've lost Cheshire. For a second, I pause, nibbling my lip as I cast my gaze around the throng. He's nowhere to be seen.

Worry immediately flares in my chest. I didn't ditch him, so I really hope that's not what he thinks. I just figured it would be easier to traverse the crowd if we weren't connected. What if I've lost him?

What if all he wanted was sex, and now he's not interested in boring little me anymore?

A lump rises in my throat, and I shiver, suddenly feeling every bit as naked as I am. The urge to turn around and go look for him instead is strong, but that would be foolish. I'm so close to achieving my goal. If I see this task through, then I can spend all night looking for Cheshire if necessary.

Or if I can't find him, I can simply go home, clothes or no clothes. If I'm broken-hearted, maybe I won't be so cold.

I shake myself physically and turn back towards the stage. First things first. Find the white rabbit.

It's harder to get closer to the court, as apparently that's where everyone wants to be. But I keep politely excusing myself and squeezing through until I can finally see my target directly, and—more importantly—he can see me.

Feeling foolish but not caring and doing it anyway, I wave at Bunny Boy. "Hello there!" I call out over the music. "Excuse me? I believe I have something of yours!"

His eyes go wide and slowly look over in my direction. I beam and wave again.

That's when Miss Royal Flush rises to her feet. My head snaps in her direction, and I realise with horror that she's looking at me, too.

She raises her hand.

The music cuts out.

Suddenly, the underground rave is very, very quiet, and everyone who can is looking in the same direction.

At me.

CHAPTER
Ten

"And WHAT is the meaning of this?" Miss Royal bellows in the deafening quiet.

I gulp, shaking so much that it's difficult to speak. "I, um, ah…"

"You *dare* to approach this court," Miss Royal continues to shout, her eyes blazing as she steps closer to me. "You *dare* to speak before you are spoken to."

Through my fear sparks just enough irritation to get my tongue going. "Now, hold on just a minute!"

As I place my hands on my hips, I remember in horror just how naked I am. But a sort of recklessness overcomes me. This is happening whether I like it or not. I might as well roll with it.

I take a quick breath and barrel on. "There's no need to raise your voice like that, really. I was only trying to help."

Miss Royal scoffs, and all her court start laughing very loudly, making me wince. Not the rabbit, though, I notice. "As if we'd need any help from *you*," she spits out. "Who even are you?"

Mr Boppers, with the strawberry vape, asked me the

exact same question. Gosh, I'm *nobody*. I wilt under her fierce gaze. My mouth opens to say just as much when I feel the weight of what's in my palm.

Maybe I'm nobody. But right now, I do have a purpose.

Making sure its chain is securely wrapped around my fingers, I hold my arm up high and let the pocket watch fall. It swings, the gold case flashing in the colourful lights.

The white rabbit gasps, his hands flying to his mouth before he warily glances at Royal Flush.

"Forgive me, Your Majesty," he says, his voice soft and sweet. "But I do believe that's my pocket watch. The one that belonged to my great-grandfather."

Pride wells up inside me. I *knew* it was a family heirloom and worth all this trouble. I smile at the rabbit, and he gives me such a look of gratitude it makes me a tad emotional.

"Well, what are you waiting for?" the queen demands with a scowl. "Give it back."

People move out of the way as I rush towards the stage. At the same time, the rabbit lurches forward onto his knees, his hand outstretched. As I thrust the watch into his grasp, I feel like a huge weight is lifted off my shoulders, and I let out a big sigh of relief. The rabbit clutches his watch to his chest and lets out a little sob.

"How did you come across such a valuable item?" Miss Royal demands. "I suppose you *stole* it, then succumbed to your guilty conscience later on."

"W-what?" I splutter incredulously, aware that everyone around me is looking at me suspiciously. "I found it on the tube! I was just—"

"And how did you get in here anyway?" she interrupts me with narrowed eyes. "Show me your key immediately!"

I gulp. "Uh...I don't have one...Your Majesty."

Her nostrils flare. At that moment, the muscular twins from the entrance step on stage, walking in eerie unison.

They take up position on either side of her and cross their arms over their burly chests.

"A party crasher!" the queen accuses.

"What? No!" I wave my hands at her, then point at her henchmen. "I came in with someone. They saw!"

Oh no, is she going to call the police on me? I feel clammy at the thought. Or maybe she'll do worse? This is her domain, after all, and it does feel a little lawless. Why invite the officials down here when she probably enacts her own justice?

I look imploringly at the twins to back me up, but they remain stoney-faced, and dread pools in my stomach. I'm not a rule-breaker! I don't want to get in trouble!

The queen scoffs again. "And where is this person you supposedly came in with? I don't think—"

"Here!" a voice cries out, and my heart skips a beat.

I and everybody else around me spins on our heels. The sight that greets me makes my heart soar.

Cheshire crashes past everyone to skid to a halt by my side. He grabs my hand, lifting it and kissing my knuckles, grinning at me like there's no one else in the room.

"I'm here," he yells proudly so everyone can hear. He turns his beaming face towards the queen. "He's with me. They saw us come in together." He gestures wildly at the twins. "He really did just want to give your friend back his watch, but he got swept up in your magnificent party whilst trying to find him."

He winks at me, and I feel ten pounds lighter. I can't believe I thought he'd abandoned me.

Although…

"YOU!" the queen roars, her face going beetroot. I wince, but Cheshire takes a breath and seems to fortify himself.

"Me," he says brazenly.

Royal Flush points a quivering finger at him. "How *dare* you show your face here."

Cheshire sighs. "Well, I did try and hide in the back whilst my boy here was all heroic and returned the pocket watch. But then you demanded I come forward, so here I am."

I'm so caught up with the fact that Cheshire called me his boy that I realise I wasn't exactly paying attention to the rest of the context.

"Huh?" I say as I glance at him. Why does Royal Flush seem to hate him?

He leans in close to me. "She hit on me, and I politely declined," he explains.

I suck in a breath and nod to show that I understand. No wonder the queen is looking thunderous.

Aaaaand that's why Cheshire didn't come with me when I pushed to the front of the crowd to reach the stage. He probably thought he'd ruin everything if he did. It's not like it's turned out great as it is, but my heart swells.

He's still here, by my side, even though it could get him in trouble. It's finally sinking in that maybe he's really *not* going to ditch me and go find somebody cooler.

Unfortunately, I don't have time to rejoice in these revelations. Miss Royal Flush looks like she's going to explode.

"The both of you!" she shrieks. "The insolence! How dare you! I should—!"

"Should *what?*" I shout back.

I'm quivering all over, and I've never felt so small. I'm barely five foot eight on a good day and she's well over six foot before the size thirteen platform heels and the added height of the stage. I feel like a tiny mouse facing up to a lion, but I don't care.

"I have spent *hours* chasing after your rabbit friend to make sure he got his watch back," I bark.

Bunny Boy clutches it to his chest again. "And I'll never be able to thank you enough for that," he says tearfully.

I give him a small nod before readdressing Miss Royal. "That's the only reason I came here and the only reason I approached the stage. I would have told you that this is the most incredible party I've ever been to, but you were more interested in being *rude* to ask. And!" I cry, getting into the swing of my rant. "If someone isn't interested in you sexually and they nicely tell you 'no', then that's the end of it! It's called consent!"

If I thought the room was quiet when the music first went off, you could hear a pin drop now. I take a couple of breaths and realise in horror what I've just done.

But then Cheshire's wrapping his arms around me and kissing my cheek. "You tell them, baby," he murmurs.

Baby?

Yeah, I actually don't mind if the queen murders me right now because I'll die very happy indeed.

"Rude?" the queen repeats, her voice as cold as ice.

I clear my throat and try not to faint. "Y-yes," I stammer. "Perhaps you ought to work on your manners."

There's a beat when I wonder if I really have gone too far. But then she erupts into peals of laughter. "My manners?" she repeats. Cheshire squeezes me, so I hold my head high and nod. "Young man, have you forgotten in whose house you are standing?"

"Not at all, Your Majesty," I assure her.

"I make the rules."

I swallow and dig my nails into my palm. "But that doesn't mean you get to abuse your power without anyone calling you out on it."

The laughter dies from her face, and I think perhaps *this* time I've pushed her over the edge. But before anything too explosive can happen, the slightly scary but handsome man in the Venetian mask hops onto the stage, a half-eaten jam tart in his hand.

"How about a game?" he asks loudly.

Miss Royal Flush blinks, then looks back at him. "A game?"

He takes a bite of his tart and nods. "Yes, a game," he says with his mouth full before swallowing. "If he wins, he's free to go."

A wicked smile spreads across the queen's face. "And if *I* win?"

The cocky man polishes off his tart by licking the crumbs off his fingers, then flashes a humourless grin at the mother of his house. "If you win, this cheeky young chap spends the night in the stocks."

I'd question if they really had a set of stocks here, but from Cheshire's sharp intake of breath, I don't need to.

Miss Royal looks delighted as she snaps her head back to pierce me with her gaze. "Well, child?" she demands. "What do you say?"

Cheshire whispers in my ear again, but this time there's not a hint of flirtiness. "You don't have to do this."

I look at him and think how he's come to my rescue again and again this evening. This is obviously his place, his 'life-style' as he called it. I loathe the thought of him being chased out because some petty man has the power to run him off out of vengeful, misplaced spite.

Also, I was really extra nice getting that pocket watch back. There was absolutely no need for the queen to pop off at me like she did. It's not fair, and I *hate* when things are unfair.

I look her dead in the eye and square my shoulders.

"Challenge accepted," I say firmly.

CHAPTER
Eleven

It occurs to me a little too late I have no idea what kind of game the queen has in mind. Hopefully, nothing too complicated because the idea of being put in stocks sounds awful. I doubt anyone would actually *hurt* me, but I would still be horribly vulnerable, especially in my state of undress. And I'm pretty sure in olden times, they encouraged people to throw food and drink at whoever was incarcerated.

Yeah. No, thank you.

But when someone I assume to be from the court thrusts a plastic flamingo into my hands, I'm at a loss. It's some sort of ghastly garden ornament, and I can't imagine what kind of event it could be necessary for.

As usual in this place, I'm thinking far too logically.

People are clearing the dance floor, and Cheshire pulls me to one side. The chess game has broken up and some of the red players seem to be positioning themselves with purpose on the illuminated area, standing with their legs apart and hands on their hips. The queen also has a plastic flamingo that she's holding by the feet. I watch on with a frown as she gives it a couple of practice swings.

Baffled, I turn to Cheshire. "What's going on?"

He shakes his head, looking equally confused. "I *think* it might be croquet."

"Croquet?" I yelp, racking my brain. It's a ball sport, right? You take it in turns to get your ball through a set of hoops, and whoever finishes the course first, wins. That sounds simple enough, but what are the flamingos for?

My question is soon answered as the man in the Venetian mask drops a couple of different coloured balls in front of the queen, and she gives one an experimental tap with the plastic flamingo's head.

"Oh, dear lord," I scoff, although I do my best to keep my voice down so only Cheshire hears. "This is ridiculous! Actual croquet mallets exist for a reason. What's the point of playing with something so awkwardly shaped?"

Cheshire gives me a sympathetic look and rubs my arm. "You're assuming she's going to play fair, are you?"

I frown at him. Before I can reply, though, one of the court members is ushering me over to the queen's side. She's got the red ball, naturally, and I'm put in front of the blue one.

At least my outfit is coordinated.

"I'm genuinely sorry about all this," someone whispers behind me. I glance over my shoulder to see the white-haired rabbit boy. He's wringing his hands, looking miserable. "You were so kind to return my watch."

I roll my shoulders and muster up a smile for him. "It really wasn't a problem," I tell him, even though we both know that's not true.

But it helps remind me that's all that actually matters. The queen can humiliate me if she wants to, but I don't know anyone here. Well, aside from Cheshire. He won't judge me if I fail.

We may have only just met, but I feel as if I do already

know him quite well. There's a delightful ache in my rear end making me recall *just* how well we got to know each other not long ago.

I blush at the memory but try and push it away for now. I won't be able to concentrate if I start daydreaming about incredible sex, and if what Cheshire said is correct, I'm going to need my wits about me.

It's clear that Miss Royal Flush plays by her own rules, and they aren't fair. But a naïve part of me thinks that because this is a competition, it has to be sportsmanlike, especially with all these people watching on. They'll see if she cheats, won't they?

Bless my heart.

"Her Majesty will play first!" the masked man declares. He's got another jam tart in his hand, and I wonder how he can possibly maintain a ripped physique like his if he spends all night eating sugary pastries.

However, his fitness regime is soon ejected from my mind as I watch Royal Flush take her first shot. She actually manages to hit the ball with the ridiculous flamingo, but it careens off to the left.

That's not a problem, though. The human chess pieces dash into action, jumping in front of the queen's ball, so it sails through three of their open legs which they're apparently using as hoops. At least the last couple of people don't reach it in time, but the crowd still erupts in applause, and she gives them a little bow.

"Bravo, Your Majesty!" the masked man cheers.

I grit my teeth. Right. I should have expected she'd pull some shenanigans. At least that means the people hoops are all aligned for me now. With a huff, I stomp over to my ball and line up the shot, focusing on the roundest part of the flamingo's head in an attempt not to send my ball off in a wild direction by accident.

I wouldn't say I'm a particularly sporty person, but I do have reasonable hand-to-eye coordination for an IT geek. I take a breath and ignore the expectant hush that's fallen over the crowd. I give myself a moment to visualise the shot… then I take it.

It's good! The ball goes flying exactly where I wanted it to!

Except I should have known that the queen and her court wouldn't stand for that.

The human hoops not only jump out of the way of my ball, but one of them kicks it off course completely.

"Oi!" I shout indignantly.

"Oh dear, what a shame," Royal Flush titters smugly. "I doubt you can win now. So I guess that makes me the victor."

"Yes, it is a shame," I say hotly, squeezing my fist around the flamingo's legs. "It's a shame that you won't even try to play fair to win. Only cowards cheat. What a hollow victory."

A collective gasp goes through the assembly, but I jut my chin out and hold my head up high. Whether she likes it or not, the queen knows I'm telling the truth.

"I've won," she says coolly.

"If you can't beat me without breaking the rules, you haven't won a single thing." I drop the flamingo on the dance floor. "So if you're not going to play fair, then I'm not going to play at all. I've done what I came here to do. I've returned the pocket watch. And now I'm leaving."

I look around for Cheshire, but I can't see him. Still, I trust he's here somewhere, so I turn and go to walk away from the queen.

Big mistake.

"GUARDS!" she bellows, making me flinch and look back. She throws her flamingo down so hard the poor thing's head snaps off. "Bring him to me!"

The muscular twins materialise out of the crowd behind

her, and I gasp in panic. But then someone grabs my wrist as well as my attention, making me turn away once more from the queen.

Cheshire's beautiful smile greets me.

"Run!" he cries.

CHAPTER
Twelve

Before I can work out what's happening, Cheshire is pulling me into the throng of onlookers. As I jerk my head to glance behind us, I realise people are spilling onto the dance-floor, their presence slowing down the court's attempts to reach me.

I feel strangely honoured, grinning as I turn back around and run hand in hand with Cheshire. Those people have no idea who I am, and some of them are still taking my side all the same. I assumed all the guests would be unwaveringly loyal to the queen, but apparently not.

"Usurpers!" Royal Flush shrieks. "Outrageous! How dare you! I won't stand for this! *Bring them to me!*"

"I think that's our cue to get out of here," Cheshire calls back at me, laughing and whooping.

My heart flips at his use of the word 'our'.

As we rush through the tunnels, the crowd parts for us. Suddenly, the flower girls are up ahead in a gaggle. They're all frantically pointing to the left, so that's the way we go. I could be wrong, as the whole night has been such a blur, but

I don't feel like I recognise anything. Is this the way I came earlier?

Behind us, the queen is still shouting, as are several members of her court, including the masked man with the jam tarts. They sound frenzied with their hunt, and I dread to think what will happen to me if they catch me.

Cheshire squeezes my hand as we continue to flee. Several feet ahead, I see the bartender in the top hat scaling one of the podium dancer's cages. He winks at us as we run by before pointing in the opposite direction. "They went that way!"

The crowd is thinning now, and I can see that we're definitely not going back the way I came into Down Street. I guess it's a different entrance, but I trust that Cheshire knows where he's going.

As we turn a corner, I look back through the throng and see the dopey guy with the party boppers trying to offer the masked man some of his mushrooms, stubbornly blocking his way. The flower girls are holding hands and dancing around the queen in a circle like something out of a children's nursery rhyme.

My heart is full. I only just met these people tonight, and yet they're willing to try and help me escape the wrath of Miss Royal Flush, even though it could cost them their place in this wonderland. I'm quite certain that's not something that happens every day.

Suddenly, we're not running on the artificial grass anymore. Cheshire yanks me back into a more regular-looking underground tunnel, dilapidated like the one I saw when I came down from Green Park station.

"Hurry!" he urges me, mischief in his voice.

We're more exposed now. As soon as the queen and her court can get through the horde, there won't be anything or anyone between us and them to protect us. But as we round a corner, a familiar figure is waiting for us.

"Oh, thank goodness!" the white rabbit cries. He holds something out to me as we stumble to a halt in front of him. "Here, take this."

He foists the black material he's holding into my hands. When I shake it out, I realise it's his tailcoat. I also notice that he's standing beside another maintenance cupboard, although I have a feeling that there aren't any mops or buckets behind this door, either.

"Thank you," I say as I gratefully shrug the jacket over my shoulders. I'm still quite naked, but having a coat on helps a lot.

Cheshire plucks my flower crown off my hair just as the rabbit removes his ears. Cheshire gives him my crown as the rabbit secures his ears on my head.

"Wha—" I utter.

Cheshire has produced his gold key from somewhere and shoves it into the lock before yanking the door open. The other side reveals a staircase going upwards like I expected it would. Voices are echoing off the tiles, getting closer. "Go!" he cries at me. "We'll lead them away."

I can't lie. I'm crushed. "You're not coming with me?" I ask in a small voice.

Cheshire swoops down and presses a firm kiss on my mouth. "I'll see you again, little one," he assures me, his eyes sparkling as they look searchingly into mine.

I don't like it, but if he distracts them, maybe I can escape. "What about you?" I hate the thought of leaving him to fend for himself.

"I'll be fine," he scoffs brazenly.

"I'll look after him," the white rabbit assures me.

Cheshire slaps my bottom and gives me one of his show-stopping grins. "Now GO!"

Our pursuers are almost on top of us, so with one last fleeting look at this dazzling stranger, I turn and sprint up the stairs, not stopping until I reach the top and crash through another door.

I expect to find myself back in Green Park. It's late, but the Jubilee line is a night tube—another reason why it's my favourite—so I could have got back on it to go home. However, I stumble out into an area that looks just as abandoned as the tunnels of Down Street below. I frown and look around as the door clicks shut behind me.

Before I even pull it, I know it's going to be locked, but I give it a try anyway. My heart sinks.

I know I didn't want to be caught and put in any stocks, but I also didn't want to leave Cheshire behind. He said he'd see me again, but I don't see how.

I can worry about that later. Right now, I don't know if anyone is running up the stairs behind me, and if they are they'll be able to come through to the surface just as I did. So I set off at a jog, following signs on the tiled walls, signalling the way out.

Modern tube stations have open entrances to them with ticket barriers people have to pass to reach the lower levels of the underground. But the signs I've been following stop abruptly, and I find myself at a security door set into a brick wall.

"I guess this is it," I say into the gloom, pushing firmly on the bar to release the door.

It swings outwards onto a quiet road, and fresh air hits me, making me shiver and inhale deeply. It's not cold, thankfully, but still I'm wearing hardly anything so it's not balmy, either.

I cross the threshold and let the door swing shut, locking behind me. Turning around, I see there's a newsagent's set into the middle arch of striking red brickwork. I came out of the left-hand side one, and the righthand one is open, a narrow one-way road going through the building.

With a small chuckle, I rub the back of my neck. "Down Street," I murmur, assuming this to be the original entrance to the long-forgotten station. "Wow."

Still wary of being caught—not to mention being highly aware of my attire—I swiftly come to the conclusion it would be better all around to hail an Uber rather than try and get myself back on the tube. I unzip the hotpants and retrieve my phone, grateful I didn't lose it or my apartment key along the way.

The car doesn't take long to arrive, and I thankfully slide into the back seat. The driver glances at me in his rear-view mirror, then chuckles. I'm sure I look ridiculous, but I don't mind. "Good night?" he asks.

I think about all the stress I've endured. Then I think of a certain beautiful smile and how those lips felt kissing mine. I gently touch my fingertips to my mouth and let a relieved laugh bubble out of me. "The best," I tell him.

And despite all the trouble I've gone through and how sad I am to have lost Cheshire, I really do mean it.

CHAPTER
Thirteen

In the early part of the twentieth century, the London Underground network started being known as the 'Tube'. This comes from the Central line, which used to be referred to as the 'Twopenny Tube' as it cost tuppence to ride back in the day.

Every year, more than one billion journeys are made through the tube, and every week, the escalators of the underground travel the equivalent distance of twice around the world.

Baker Street has ten platforms, the most of any tube station. The Victoria line was originally going to be called the Viking line. Lord only knows why they didn't opt for that instead.

And in total, there are forty-nine abandoned or 'ghost' stations hidden under the surface of the city of London.

But only one of those holds my heart.

I sleepwalk my way through most of the rest of the week-end. I try and be productive by unpacking some more of my boxes and making a new flatpack set of drawers. But my mind keeps wandering back to Down Street and to a smile that's doing its best to haunt me.

At times, I manage to convince myself that it was just one unbelievably crazy and magical night and that I need to move on. But more often than not I start fantasising about finding my way back there into Cheshire's arms.

Who knows if he's even going to go back after the queen was so mad at him, though? Perhaps aligning himself with me will push her over the edge. I *hate* the idea of him being put into stocks just as much as I did when it was my head on the line.

Not to mention that I don't know how frequent those parties are. They could be every night or once a month or once a *year.* And I don't have a token to get inside. There's no telling if the same ones are used each time or if the locks are changed for every party and new keys sent out to patrons.

My final morose thought is that the next event could be held at an entirely different venue.

It all seems pretty bleak.

On Sunday evening, I sit on my clean but threadbare carpet, sipping screw-top red wine from one of the only glasses I had at uni that didn't chip or shatter on me during my various moves. Pieces of a bedside table lie around me, but I've lost enthusiasm for the task.

For the sake of my mental health, I should probably forget all about finding Cheshire again and just lock up the memories I have of us that night in a box in my heart where I can keep them safe. But the hopeless romantic in me is clinging to the fact that he said he'd find me.

Realistically, I know it was only one night—only a few hours, when you really think about it. That shouldn't be enough to addle my brain the way it has, but here we are.

Eventually, I give up on the furniture, swap wine for water, and drag myself to bed. I spend an embarrassing amount of time trying to search online for hot young guys called Cheshire, but surprisingly, with no last name, I don't come up with anything useful.

Shocking, I know.

I guess I must have fallen asleep at some point, because my alarm wakes me up at the crack of dawn. I groan in protest, but I only allow myself one smack of the snooze button before resigning myself to my fate and heading to the shower.

This is the start of my new, exciting London life. I can't let my melancholy over a boy hold me back. Even if he was handsome and kind and daring and funny, and…

Gah! Stop!

I try having a cheeky wank under the hot water, but although the release is pleasant, as soon as my high ebbs away, I'm back to reality.

One look at the time soon clears my thoughts, however. *I'm late!* Even after setting my alarm early and laying out my clothes the night before, I've let myself get behind. I didn't realise how long I'd let myself daydream about Cheshire in the shower, and now I'm in real danger of showing up on my first day a sweaty, gasping mess.

Somehow, I manage to throw my clothes on, grab all my stuff, and run out the door with a cereal bar in record time. The tube station is a few minutes' walk, but I run the whole way to try and make up for lost time. I had the presence of mind to grab my deodorant before I left, so if worst comes to worst, I'll nip in the loos and reapply it.

Better dishevelled than late, I reason as I run down the escalator to the platform.

The travel gods are on my side as a train pulls up a matter of seconds after I skid to a halt. I chug some water and do my best to slow my heart down as I board with all the other commuters.

It's packed, but I put my noise-cancelling earbuds in and crank up my music to try and find a little calmness to see me through the journey. By the time I get off at London Bridge, I've had my cereal bar and the rest of my water. I even used my reflection in the tube carriage window to tame my hair.

"You can do this," I mutter to myself as I make my way to ground level again. The words don't really resonate with me, but then I take a slow, deep breath and imagine Cheshire saying them to me like he did on Friday night.

Suddenly, I feel like I can take on the world.

I had my interviews here, so I know my way as I buzz the front door and get a visitor's pass like I'd been instructed. I need a photo to get proper ID, so that will happen later.

After such a hectic sprint here, I opt to take the elevator rather than the stairs in an effort not to get any sweatier than I already have done. It also gives me the chance to take a few more breaths and centre myself.

This is going to be a great job. I was so excited when they made me the offer. I know IT isn't everyone's idea of a good time, but I love programming and debugging and all the quiet tasks I fill my day with. Besides, this is an events management company, so their whole ethos is having fun.

The office is sleek and modern with employee well-being in mind. So there's proper food in the cafeteria, alcoholic drinks provided every Friday afternoon, bean bags in the breakroom, massage chairs, a small company gym, and you're even allowed to bring your pets to work with you so long as they are reasonably well behaved.

I'm sure it's going to take a long time to see anything quite as crazy as the kind of shindig the Haus of Cards put on, but for work, this is certainly a lot better than the dreary place I'd been stuck at since uni.

I push through the doors that separate the office space from the elevator hallway. By some miracle, I'm a few minutes early. I take a fortifying breath, then approach the main open office space.

"Alexander!" my new manager cries. Her name is Frances, and she immediately gets up from her desk to greet me, curls bouncing as she strides over to shake my hand.

"Um, actually, is it okay to go by Alex?" I ask.

"Of course," she says without missing a beat. "We're the IT department, so we have the luxury of setting up our own email addresses and the like. Alex it is."

I glance around as a few people give me friendly waves. But then I look down at my smart trousers, shirt, and tie and feel just as out of place as I did on Friday night. "Oh, everyone's so casual."

Frances makes a dismissive noise. "You dress however you feel comfortable, hun. I think it's nice to make an effort, especially on your first day. But you'll soon realise that Jerry over there wears shorts and flip-flops even if it's snowing. You're here to help the company run smoothly, not put on a fashion parade."

The tension eases from my shoulders. "Thanks," I say, feeling a little less like a nerd.

Jeans and a T-shirt are more my usual style, although after losing that pair on Friday night, I'll have to try and get some more so I'm not wearing the same pair all the time. *I don't want to get a reputation like Jerry,* I think with a half-smile.

"The big boss wanted to say hello before I started putting you through the wringer," Frances says as I follow her through the cubicles divided by walls that come up to my chest. It means everyone has some privacy, but they're not lonely, either. I see that it's okay to decorate the walls with personal items, and I wonder what I could bring in tomorrow to make my cubby a little more my own.

I know I've only just walked into the building, but I can't help but feel like I'm going to belong here.

"Here we are," Frances says, stopping in front of a frosted door. There are a few along this wall, presumably for upper management. "It's nothing to worry about. Mr Grimalkin just wants to show his face before you get overwhelmed on your first day. When you're done, I'll be right over there." She points to the desk from where she came.

"Thank you," I tell her sincerely.

Hopefully, this guy won't be some out-of-touch bloke who calls us every ten minutes, only to be told to turn his laptop off and on again. I smooth down my shirt and straighten the strap on my messenger bag. I've already got the job. There's no reason to be nervous. I knock firmly on the door.

"Come in," a confident voice calls from the other side. So I turn the handle, step over the threshold, and…

And stop.

Behind the desk…is Cheshire.

My jaw drops as the door swings shut behind me. He looks a little different in a long-sleeved T-shirt, but that killer smile is exactly how I remember it. Behind his desk in the corner is a tall cat tree where a fluffy kitty pokes their head out from the top level to look at me. On the desk itself is a laptop, a succulent plant, a mug with paw prints painted on it, and…

And the clothes that I lost, folded up in a neat pile, my blue flower crown resting on top. Nestled on the crown is a light blue cat collar, the front of which is propped up on the flowers so I can just about read the silver name tag glinting in the office light.

'Alex'.

I look between that and Cheshire's gleeful face a couple of times, trying to make words form. Nothing happens.

Cheshire leans forward, placing his elbows on the desk, lacing his hands together, and resting his chin on the backs of his fingers.

"Hello, little one," he says with a grin.

———

Thank you so much for reading Alex and Cheshire's story! If you enjoyed it, please consider leaving a review on your favourite bookish site. It helps us indie authors a lot! And if you'd like to discover more of my fairy tale adaptations as well as other contemporary books (as HJ Welch), turn the page!

———

Thank you to my team!
    Cover Design: Joe Satoria
    Editing: Meg Cooper
    Proof Reading: Tanja Ongkiehong
    Special thanks (for the title!): Ed Davies
    Love and support: Hubby and our cats

Wild Ride

When Red is chased into the woods, he seeks sanctuary at his estranged grandma's house. He doesn't expect to be rescued by his older brother's best friend, the man he was always madly in love with. Could Hunter be the Daddy of Red's wildest dreams? Especially when he unlocks a secret passion of Red's for beautiful lingerie. There's still a threat lurking in the woods, though, and Hunter realises he'll do anything to protect his beautiful boy.

Three

When three shy best friends sign up to a dating app to finally get some by the end of the year, they don't expect to all fall for the same gorgeous, slightly scary-looking Daddy. The only solution? Let him choose who he wants to bed. Except he doesn't. Daddy Wolf wants to spoil each little piggy, one after another. But when danger comes calling, will their love for each other be enough to save them all?
Includes Halloween bonus scene!

Nine Lives

When Charlie suddenly finds himself homeless and penniless, he decides to sell the only thing left he owns. Himself. For the very first time. Lucky for him he stumbles across Miller, the own of a London kink club, who saves him from those who would take advantage of him. As Miller discovers his inner Daddy, he also unlocks Charlie's kitten alter-ego. But with both their families meddling, will new love be enough to keep them together?

Click here to get the Daddy's Fairy Tales Box Set

door, will Joshua and Darius's blossoming love be strong enough to save each other?

————

A Right Royal Affair

Nobody knows that Prince James of the United Kingdom is bisexual, and as he's sixth in line to the throne, it needs to stay that way. But when he meets the cheeky, outrageously gay Essex boy, Theo Glass, everything could change. Against his better judgement, James asks Theo to help him put on a royal charity ball to remember. Can they resist their mutual attraction for a whole week alone in a picturesque castle, or will true love bloom?

————

Hair Out of Place

Raphael d'Oro is a secret prince who has spent his entire life exiled in a London penthouse. But now he's in a race against time to get back to his tiny European nation to claim the throne that's rightfully his and save his people. Good thing he has his insanely hot older bodyguard to take care of him. But Griff Thompson would never want someone as inexperienced as Raphie, would he? Even *if* they keep finding themselves in places with only one bed…

Click here for the Fairy Tale Collection eBook

Click here for the Fairy Tale Collection audio

JACKED UP BY HELEN JULIET

Little thief. Big problem.

JACK

When some billionaire tries to mess with my family, I decide to take personal revenge and break into his London penthouse when he's abroad to steal some compensation. The issue? He's not only very much home, but he's *huge.* Even worse, he's gorgeous and too bloody cheerful. Rather than call the police, he suggests that I stay until I've fixed what I've damaged. It's only for a few days, but I start to realise this guy isn't the villain I thought he was. In fact, he might be everything I've ever dreamed I could never have.

FELIX

It's only a little light kidnapping, so I don't feel too bad. Besides, this small, grumpy thief I've caught is too adorable. I'm drawn to his broken soul. I want to protect him from his troubles and dominate him in the bedroom. We're perfect for each other but he's determined to believe that he doesn't belong in my world. Can I convince him to stay? Or is this fairy tale doomed before it's even begun?

Jacked Up is a super steamy, standalone MM gay romance novel featuring one hell of a size difference, a romantic date in the clouds, a singing and matchmaking parrot, past wounds long overdue for healing, and a guaranteed HEA with absolutely no cliffhanger.

Click here for the Jacked Up eBook

PINE COVE BOX SET BY HJ WELCH

Welcome to Pine Cove, where true love lives happily ever after! **This 2000 page box set contains all six novels as well as all five companion short stories.**

Click here to get the Pine Cove eBook bundle

Click here to get the Pine Cove audio bundle

———

Safe Harbor

Robin Coal needs a fake boyfriend for his high school reunion. He asks his housemate: a gorgeous, totally straight ex-Marine. What could go wrong? There's only one bed, and Dair might not be so straight after all... When Robin's past threatens their future, only Dair can save him.

———

Sweet Spot

It's Halloween and Robin has prepared a sexy little surprise for his boyfriend Dair when he gets home from work. Hold on to your horses, Marine!

———

Troubled Waters

Bodyguard Scout Duffy doesn't know what's worse: the fact that his scorching one-night-stand, Emery Klein, is his bratty new client, or the fact that he doesn't even remember Scout. But Emery's life is in danger thanks to his out and proud charity work, and once he finally recognizes Scout, their chemistry in undeniable.

———

Homeward Bound

Swift Coal just found out he's a father, and his daughter (and her cranky cat) are coming to stay. His best friend's younger brother, Micha Perkins, has nowhere to go and a wrongfully tattered reputation. He's relieved when Swift asks him to be a live-in babysitter. He just has to hide his lifelong crush. Easy, because Swift is straight—right?

———

Bright Horizon

With sixteen years between them, baker Ben Turner and lawyer Elias Solomon have no idea their crush is mutual. But when Ben inherits his long-lost family's estate and becomes an overnight millionaire, Elias swears to protect the innocent younger man from the vultures circling him. To unravel the mystery of the inheritance, they must go to England to confront Ben's estranged relatives…and their feelings for each other.

———

Crossed Paths

Raj Bhat is done living in the shadows. It's time for him to take charge of his own destiny and tell the man he's fallen for how he really feels.

———

Midnight Sky

It's the night before New Year's Eve. Taylan Demir is all alone, and he's just lost his dog. Except when his handsome customer, Hudson Perkins, comes to his rescue, Taylan doesn't just get his dog back. He's suddenly got a hot date, and maybe someone to kiss when the clock strikes midnight.

———

Memory Lane

Angel Shields saved Jay Coal's life in high school, and Jay has secretly loved his straight best friend ever since. Now Angel's back in town with amnesia after a suspicious work accident and it's Jay's turn to rescue him. He pretends to be Angel's fiancé to see him in the hospital, but with his scrambled-up memory, Angel's not sure it's fictional after all. He just knows he loves Jay more than ever.

———

Thin Ice

Kamran's ex broke his heart, tricked him into aiding a bank robbery, and now he wants him to do one last job. There's only one way to say no: seek the protective custody of the biggest, grumpiest FBI agent ever, Lee Marshall. And pretend to be his boyfriend for a week-long family reunion in their giant mansion. Wait, what?

———

Calm Shores

Gorgeous, sophisticated Dante walks into Oliver's bar and orders…a boyfriend?! Dante needs a man to keep his mother from setting him

back up with his awful, cheating ex, and Oliver is up for the
challenge.

———

Fresh Snow

Emery Klein is throwing the best Christmas party ever, but his
fiancé, Scout Duffy, and all their friends have something more
exciting in mind.

———

*Each Pine Cove book can be read as a stand alone and has its own happy
ever after. But if you read the whole series, you'll see a lot of familiar faces!*

Click here to get the Pine Cove eBook bundle

Click here to get the Pine Cove audio bundle

Spark

The last thing Joey Sullivan wants is to go back to his homophobic family, but he's penniless and has no choice. Recently single and heartbroken Gabe Robinson loves the town Joey hates. As a librarian and voluntary firefighter, he's used to helping people. When Joey gets a lucky break out of state, Gabe doesn't hesitate to take him on a road trip. The sparks that fly between them have to be just temporary, though. Joey can't wait to leave town and his family are eager to kick him out the door. Can Gabe's love save him from ending up on the streets? *Contains bonus epilogue.*

Burn

Songwriter Raiden Jones never thought he'd need a bodyguard. But when a malicious hacker starts destroying his career and threatening his life, he finds himself desperately in need of protection. That means ex-Marine Levi Patterson is stuck on tour with the bratty Raiden, their friction quickly turning sexual. Bisexual Levi is firmly in the closet and Raiden's never thought of being with a man before, but the chemistry is too fierce to ignore. Will the hacker ruin everything before they can work through their differences? *Contains bonus epilogue.*

Steam

Bad boy movie star Trent Charles is in need of an image makeover. Ashby Wilcott wants some peace and quiet after his ex-boyfriend cheated on him. They both find themselves in a remote ski resort, but Ashby refuses to fall for hot-as-hell Trent. Good thing Trent is straight, because Ashby is done with trouble makers. Except when Trent rescues Ashby from a sleaze, they find themselves pretending to be boyfriends for a wedding weekend. Ashby awakes a longing in Trent he's never felt before, and Ashby realizes Trent has a heart of gold. But can this fling last longer than the melting snow when there's a creep determined to tear them apart?

Blaze

Reyse Hickson might be an international pop sensation, but he's also forced to remain in the closet thanks to his homophobic record label. When gorgeous Corey Sheppard saves Reyse from a mugging, Reyse can't resist falling into his bed, if only for one night. However, a family emergency calls Reyse home, and it seems like the perfect chance for him and Corey to steal some secret time together. But it can't last. Reyse's label would never allow it. Can Reyse and Corey walk away from the best thing that's ever happened to either of them? Or is this love worth going down in a blaze of glory? *Contains bonus epilogue.*

Each Homecoming Hearts book can be read as a stand alone and has its own happy ever after. But if you read the whole series, you'll see familiar faces returning, and enjoy the spectacular ending of Blaze even more!

Click here to get the Homecoming Hearts eBook bundle

PADDLE CREEK DADDIES 1-4 BOX SET BY HJ WELCH

Welcome to the underdog town of Paddle Creek, where it's always the quiet ones who get up to the best kind of trouble! Join the boys, princesses, littles, lambs – you name it! – of Paddle Creek College as they meet their Daddies and find true love…with a little help from the colorful locals, of course.

This 900 page box set features the first four full length novels of the ongoing series as well as a previously unpublished 9K word bonus prologue to Four Play.

Click here to get the Paddle Creek Daddies 1-4 eBook bundle

———

ONE – Heaven Sent

Two rival jocks. One adorable nerd. A bet that changes everything.

Seth is the captain of the Paddle Creek Panthers. Marty is the football team's slacker clown. Gabe is the shy nerd who's caught both their attention. They have nothing in common…until they get pulled into a scheme by the college bully. If Seth and Marty don't graduate, they could all lose everything unless Gabe can get the jocks' grades up. But when sparks fly between all three, sweet Gabe finds himself with two hot Daddies desperate to take his V card… and his heart.

TWO – Yes, Sir

Two men. Two secrets. Can true love set them free?

Benedict is a professor at Paddle Creek College with a hidden desire to be called Sir by willing subs. His new younger TA, Jackson, has the body of a gym rat, but under his clothes, satin and lace are waiting to be discovered. Jackson has no idea what calling his new boss Sir does to him. However, it's nothing compared to when they start some serious role playing, and he calls him Daddy as well. But Benedict is leaving at the end of the year, so their relationship can never be anything more than a secret fling…right?

THREE – Little Pleasures

One jaded Daddy. One brand new boy. A fake relationship that becomes all too real.

Xander has been in love with his older brother's best friend forever. Ruben has all but given up trying to find a sweet little to Daddy. But when a lie gets out of hand, Ruben suddenly finds himself pretending to be Xander's boyfriend to protect him at an awful family wedding. As time goes on, Ruben can't help but encourage Xander's dinosaur loving little side out, and soon enough nothing is make believe anymore.

FOUR – Four Play

Three hungry wolves. One pretty little lamb. The hunt for love is on.

Former soldiers Rick and Trey are married and devoted to their boyfriend, Brady. Primal play is what gets their blood pumping. When Brady wants to try being the hunter for once, he discovers bratty Harper is a natural at being chased. However, these three hot men aren't the only thing Harper is running from. Under this young man's bravado lurk wounds that need healing, and Daddy Rick is determined to add this sweet and sassy lamb to his wolf pack. But when Harper's past catches up to him, will four be the magic number to save him?

BONUS PROLOGUE – Be Four

Two Daddies in search of a boy. But is it for one night or forever?

After swapping military life for married life, Rick and Trey continue to enjoy an open relationship where they can both dominate in the bedroom. But when they meet gorgeous Brady at a steamy party, they soon realize that what they have is bigger than just a one-night stand. [Please note: This short story is set two years after the prologue of Four Play and two years before Chapter One of the same book. It can be read before or after Four Play—whatever you prefer!]

Each Paddle Creek Daddies book can be read as a stand alone with its own happily ever after. But if you read the whole series, you'll soon spot the grumpy owner of the cat café, a mischievous trash panda with a heart of gold, and a slightly terrifying librarian who may or may not be an actual witch. Not to mention familiar Daddies and boys!

Click here to get the Paddle Creek Daddies 1-4 eBook bundle

NIM

I'm a terrible Daddy. My last kitten told me that. Words and emotions are tough for me. But when the perfect boy drops into my lap, how can I refuse? Rescuing strays is what I do. It's only so long that I can resist this beautiful kitten and his bubbly personality. But someone in town has it out for me and my fellow bikers, branding us troublemakers. I can't let Jessie be dragged down with me, not when it puts everything he's worked so hard for at risk. I swore I'd do anything to protect him. Even if that means letting him go.

Hell's Kitten is a steamy, standalone MM romance. It's the fifth book in the **Paddle Creek Daddies series**, where it's always the quiet ones who get up to the best kind of trouble. This book features first-time kitten play, two broken hearts, a cheerleading championship, far too many black cats to count, enough love for nine whole lives, and a guaranteed HEA with absolutely no cliffhanger.

Click here to get Paddle Creek Daddies #5: Hell's Kitten eBook

PADDLE CREEK DADDIES #6: MAKE BELIEVE BY HJ WELCH

One scorned doll. His enemy's straight father. Is it revenge, or could this be true love?

KADENCE

Secretly fooling around with a closeted D-bag like Logan McKenna was always a bad idea. So I ended it, much to his fury. Retribution is swift, and his humiliation of me is devastating. I can't let him get away with it, though. That's why a chance meeting with his supposedly straight father seems like the perfect revenge scheme. I'll seduce him with my alter ego, Kiki the living doll, and once I have some juicy photos, I'll ruin the entire family.

Except Rafferty McKenna is nothing like his son. He's kind,

thoughtful, tender, and not to mention hot as all sin. I've been broken down by not only his son but my homophobic family and my callous ex-Daddy. But as Rafferty starts to piece me back together with love and care, can I really go through with this plan of mine?

RAFFERTY

When a living doll throws himself at me, it doesn't matter that he's a boy not a girl. He's simply *mine* and I can do whatever I want with him. One passionate encounter at a party won't do, so I invite him to stay with me for a weekend, but even that's not enough. He makes me feel alive in a way my failed marriage never has. However, as our connection gets deeper, I can tell he's keeping secrets. This is just a fling, and I can't seriously be thinking about burning my whole life down for something that's not even real. Right?

*Make Believe is a steamy, standalone MM romance. It's the sixth book in the **Paddle Creek Daddies series**, where it's always the quiet ones who get up to the best kind of trouble. This book features Kiki the fabulous, bratty doll who will do anything for her Daddy, an extremely naughty conference call, a romantic picnic, two hearts in need of mending, plenty of secrets that need to come out, and a guaranteed HEA with absolutely no cliffhanger.*

Content warnings: This book features a scene of consensual sharing, as well as a loveless marriage with both husband and wife knowingly cheating on one another. However, Kadence and Rafferty never cheat on each other.

Click here to get Paddle Creek Daddies #6: Make Believe eBook

About the Author

Helen Juliet is a British author of contemporary MM fairy tale adaptations, including the international bestselling Beauty and the Beast retelling, Thorn in His Side. She lives just outside of London with her husband and three balls of fluff that occasionally pretend to be cats.

She began writing at an early age, later honing her craft online in the world of fanfiction on sites like Wattpad. Fifteen years and over half a million words later, she sought out original MM novels to read. By the end of 2016 she had written her first book of her own, and in 2017 she achieved her lifelong dream of becoming a full-time author.

When she's not writing she's usually dancing, singing, filming music videos, taking long walks, working on jigsaw puzzles, drinking prosecco, or talking about Eurovision.

She also writes contemporary American small town MM series as HJ Welch, including Pine Cove, Homecoming Hearts, and Paddle Creek Daddies.

––––––––

You can contact Helen Juliet via social media:

Newsletter (never miss a release!) – https://www.subscribepage.com/helenjuliet

Website (with FREE original stories) – www.helen-juliet.com

Facebook Group – Helen's Jewels

Facebook Page – @helenjulietauthor
Instagram – @helenjwrites
Twitter – @helenjwrites
Book Bub – @helenjuliet